"Uh-oh," Ronnie said, giggling.

Ace wiped his lips with his napkin. "What's wrong?"

"I don't usually drink much because wine…um, it puts me in the mood."

Ace smirked and laughed along with her. "If I'd known that's all I had to do, we could have just stayed in the hotel room with a bottle of wine."

"How long will it take us to get back there?" she asked, circling the rim of her glass with her finger.

"Too long," he said. "Besides, we don't have to go back right away. We've got this room all to ourselves. No one will interrupt us."

"Are you sure? What about Phillipe?"

"He's not coming back. Come here."

Ronnie got out of her seat and slowly walked over to straddle Ace. "Phillipe forgot to tell you what goes best with Château Margaux," she whispered.

"Oh, yeah. And just what is that?" he asked, slipping his hands around her waist and cupping her backside.

Wrapping her arms around his neck, she suckled on his earlobe, then whispered in his ear. "Me."

Books by Robyn Amos

Kimani Romance

Enchanting Melody
Sex and the Single Braddock
Cosmic Rendezvous
Romancing the Chef

ROBYN AMOS

worked a multitude of day jobs while pursuing a career in writing after graduating from college with a degree in psychology. Then she married her real-life romantic hero, a genuine rocket scientist, and she was finally able to live her dream of writing full-time. Since her first book was published in 1997, Robyn has written tales of romantic comedy and suspense for several publishers, including Kensington, Harlequin Books, and HarperCollins. A native to the Washington, D.C., metropolitan area, Robyn currently resides in Odenton, Maryland.

ROMANCING
the
Chef

ROBYN AMOS

KIMANI™
ROMANCE

KIMANI PRESS™

ISBN-13: 978-0-373-86194-1

ROMANCING THE CHEF

Copyright © 2011 by Robyn Amos

www.kimanipress.com

Printed in U.S.A.

ROMANCING
the
Chef

Chapter 1

Veronica Howard stretched her aching muscles. Her step aerobics class had been especially rigorous today, and she knew she'd pay the price tomorrow.

Ronnie was thirty years old and a former couch potato. So when it came to exercise, her body was in a constant state of rebellion.

"After you've done it for a while, you'll start to love it," her best friend, Cara Gray, a former fitness instructor at the trendy Tower Vista health club, had often told her. But Ronnie had been working out seriously for over a year… and she still hated it.

Ronnie headed from the locker room to the club's juice bar, The Big Squeeze, where she and Cara hung out after their workouts. The state-of-the-art gym in Bethesda, Maryland, was a bit of a drive from her new town house in Washington, D.C., but it was worth it to keep up their tradition. Without Cara's constant pep talks, Ronnie would have quit a dozen different times already.

Even though Cara was now helping her husband, A.J., run their computer consulting business, the women still met at the gym three times a week. But her best friend didn't need the workouts. Cara's years of physical fitness had apparently made her body fat resistant even after three kids. But Ronnie, who worked with food for a living, needed to exert herself to stay fit.

As Ronnie entered the juice-bar area, she saw that Cara was already waiting for her. Cara had placed a shot glass filled with a ruby-red juice at her seat. It looked like blended berries, so Ronnie picked up the glass and filled her mouth. As soon as the thick liquid touched her tongue, she nearly gagged.

"Ugh. What the heck is this?" she sputtered. "It tastes like…beets."

Cara laughed at Ronnie's yuck-face. "And hello to you, too." She nodded to Ronnie's half-empty glass. "It's a special blend of carrots, beetroot and grapefruit juice, so good call on the beets."

Ronnie wiped her tongue on her napkin. "And you thought I would like this *why?*"

"Because it's good for you," Cara said with a mischievous grin. "I figured you were ready to kick things up a notch."

Ronnie shoved the glass across the table. "Well, I guess I'm not, because I'm not drinking any more of this."

"Ron-nie! You're a chef. Your highly trained palate should be able to handle a little beetroot."

"Honey, I may have a newly skinny body, but that doesn't mean I have skinny taste buds." She swiveled her neck, feeling her curly ponytail swinging at her nape. "If there's one thing I've learned in the last few months, it's everything in moderation."

She eyed the offending glass. "And some things in *nada-ration*."

Cara rolled her eyes, having finally learned to ignore Ronnie's affinity for making up words.

Ronnie caught a glimpse of her reflection in the mirrored panels behind the bar. It still shocked her to see that her round frame had been replaced with an hourglass. As a chef, she'd worn her extra weight as a badge of honor—a testimony to the quality of her food. For years she'd told all who would listen, "If I lost weight, people would think my food wasn't any good."

She'd been a member of Tower Vista for as long as her friend had worked there, but it was only recently that she'd gotten serious about working out. The good old days had been all about massages, dips in the hot tub and fruity juice-bar drinks—all the perks of belonging to an upscale gym without the perspiration or sore muscles. But after coping with some harsh realities in recent years, Ronnie had realized it was time for a few drastic changes.

Her dream of opening her own restaurant had finally come to fruition, and she'd lost nearly eighty pounds. But the most significant weight she'd lost was the one-hundred-eighty-pound no-good ex-boyfriend she'd finally cut loose.

Now she was happily single, and the only male she needed was her German shepherd, Baxter. Baxter provided affection, security and above all…loyalty—the one thing she'd never been able to get from a man.

"Fine. You're off the hook for today." Cara took back the red shot and downed it in one gulp. "But I'm not giving up the battle. I'm going to turn you into a health nut sooner rather than later."

It's never going to happen, Ronnie thought, but she kept that fact to herself. When she'd decided to get in shape,

Cara had been beside herself with glee. Even though she no longer trained professionally, she'd taken Ronnie's weight loss on like a job, mapping out a strict regimen of diet and exercise. Now, even though Ronnie was happy with her current figure, Cara was still trying to push her further and further into the realm of fitness fanaticism.

"Yeah, good luck with that. In the meantime, I've got some news."

Her friend's eyes lit up. "What kind of news? Are you ready to start dating again?"

Ronnie rolled her eyes. Sure, three years was a long dry spell without a man, but she still hadn't reacquired her thirst. And the time on her own had done her a lot of good.

"Believe me, this has nothing to do with any man. I've been invited to participate in another Gourmet TV *Food Fight*."

Cara blinked. "That's great, Ronnie, but you do those all the time."

Ronnie smiled. "Yes, but this one is special. It's the first ever *All-Star Food Fight*. They're taking the top winners from the last two years and pitting us against each other in a three-part challenge. The prize is one hundred thousand dollars!"

Cara's eyes widened with surprise. "You're kidding me. That's ten times what you usually win."

"I know, and that's not all. Each round takes place in a fabulous place—Las Vegas, Hawaii and Paris."

Cara clutched a hand to her heart, her almond eyes taking on a dreamy expression. "You lucky girl. I've always wanted to visit Paris."

Ronnie's posture collapsed. "Well, there's no guarantee that I'll make it to Paris. The challenge starts out with five contestants. With eliminations after the first two rounds, only the top three will get to go to Paris."

Her friend, loyal to the end, waved off her concerns. "Oh, don't worry. I know you'll make it to the final three. One, because none of those chefs have the creativity and flair you have. And two, because I'm so going to visit you in Paris for the finale."

Ronnie released a tense breath, and Cara reached across the table to give her hand a reassuring pat. "Crave has been open for almost two years, and it's already received four-stars. You have nothing to worry about."

"Thanks for the vote of confidence, but there's going to be some pretty stiff competition. In fact, against most of these celebrity chefs, I definitely qualify as an underdog."

"Really? Who *are* the other chefs?"

"First, there's the queen bee herself, Etta Foster."

Etta Foster, a cross between Martha Stewart and Sarah Lee, was a household name. She had the most extensive line of cookware and frozen foods of any chef in the business. That was aside from her franchise of cooking shows on Gourmet TV. Yet despite her vast culinary empire, she still evoked the down-home image of a Southern grandma baking in her country kitchen.

Cara shrugged. "Etta Foster is a powerhouse, but she's old-fashioned. Your modern approach will blow her out of the water."

"Okay, but I'll still have to face off with Ann Le Marche and Stewart Compton."

Her friend, who only watched GTV when Ronnie was on it, was unimpressed. "I've never even heard of them."

"Well, I'm certain you've heard of my biggest competition, Ace Brown."

Cara gasped. "Ace Brown? The Sexy Chef himself?

Now you're talking. Finally a chance to prove yourself against your old culinary-school rival. Wiping the floor with him will put the icing on your victory."

Ronnie laughed. She and Ace had always been friends, but there had been an air of unspoken competition between them. They'd gone head-to-head many times in school, but unfortunately he had more points in the win column than she did. Since graduation, his career had grown to overshadow hers entirely.

Ace had been on the fast track, landing himself a show on Gourmet TV called *The Sexy Chef* soon after building his reputation on the Manhattan restaurant scene. His show had focused on romantic meals prepared from ingredients considered to be aphrodisiacs. Despite the show's popularity, when his contract was up, he'd decided to leave television to travel the world.

Ronnie hadn't seen Ace in nearly two years, and she couldn't help but feel a tad excited to show off her recent successes.

Every woman in culinary school had had a crush on Ace, herself included. But since she'd had a boyfriend at the time, Ronnie had been able to pretend she was the lone female on earth immune to his charms. As a result, they'd become good friends.

Ace's face flashed in her mind. Back then he'd had a full head of curly hair, a clean-shaven baby face and a leanly muscled body. When Ronnie had started catching *The Sexy Chef* on GTV, she'd noticed that Ace had become so buff he'd needed to cut the sleeves off his chef's jacket to free his massive guns. He'd also shaved his head and grown a neat mustache and goatee.

Combine his smoking hot physique and his natural charm in front of the camera, and you had the recipe for sexy. His show had been aptly named, and Ronnie suspected that when it had been on the air, his female viewers tuned in more for the tasty sight of Ace than for his romance-inspired haute cuisine.

Ronnie had never really been immune to his charms, but a guy like Ace had his pick of women. So why would he have gone for the pretty but pleasantly plump version of her? There were plenty of men who'd appreciated her voluptuous curves. But judging by the swarm of skinny women that had surrounded Ace, she didn't have any reason to believe he was one of them.

Therefore, it had been easier for her to pretend that she wasn't interested. To sell the lie she'd joked that she was more woman than he could handle.

"Wow—" Cara said, snapping her fingers in front of Ronnie's face "—the mere mention of Ace Brown sends you into a dream state."

"I wasn't daydreaming. It's been a while since I last saw him. I'm hoping he'll be thrown off his game when he gets a load of all this," she said, presenting her body with a flourish worthy of Vanna White.

Cara laughed. "I'm certain he'll be so intimidated by your hot body and restaurant success that he'll lose all ability to function. Then you can whisk the floor with him."

"How can I expect him to be impressed with my one little restaurant opening? He has two bistros in New York, a television show in syndication and a new cookbook coming out. The only way I'm going to earn his respect is by kicking his butt in the *Food Fight*."

Ace Brown stacked his canapés, delicately balancing Serrano ham, roasted tomatoes and shaved Parmesan cheese on thinly sliced crostini. He garnished each layer with a leaf of cilantro and carried the platter out to his guests waiting in the living room of his Manhattan loft.

He'd spent the majority of his career creating dishes for two, but tonight his apartment was filled with six of his closest friends—all of them foodies and one of them his sous chef for the upcoming competition.

"I can't believe you've just returned to the country, and you're already running off again," Devon said as Ace held the tray out to her. A polished hotshot lawyer, she wore her short hair slicked to her scalp, light makeup and a casual pantsuit.

"That's right," her husband, Ace's oldest friend, Spence, said. "We've gone almost six months without a decent meal. Now you're asking us to hold on for another three weeks?" A light-skinned pretty boy, Spence had done his friend a favor when he'd married Devon. Ace did a lot better with women without the added competition.

Ace offered the tray to the remaining couples in the room, his sous chef Marcel and his wife, Simone, and Garett, his publicist, and Garett's date du jour.

"Relax. Tonight I've planned a feast that should tide all of you over until Marcel and I return home from battle."

Garett squirmed in his seat. "I still think we should have accepted the television deal. Gourmet TV offered you a minimum of six episodes to cook your signature dishes in front of a live audience. You're getting too big for these little competition shows." Garett slapped the knee of the girl he'd brought. "Talk some sense into him, sweetheart."

Ace exchanged smirks with Marcel and Spence because he knew they were all thinking the same thing. One, Garett had called his date sweetheart because he probably didn't remember her name. And two, he'd chosen a perfect stranger to reason with Ace over a roomful of friends he'd known for years.

The beautiful Asian woman smiled at him tentatively.

"I'm sorry, Garett—" Ace said, letting her off the hook, "—I'm just not ready to commit to another TV show. I want to promote my upcoming cookbook, and then see what happens after that. I've been driving in the fast lane for so long. It would be nice to take some time to regroup."

"I thought that's what you were doing on your extended vacation," Garett said, raking his fingers through the dark locks that hung just below his ears.

"That was work. In addition to researching my book, you had me doing press everywhere I stopped." Garett always wanted more, and he always wanted it now.

The two men had become friends years ago when they were both starting out their careers. Back then they'd had two things in common—skirt chasing and a driving hunger for success.

Since Ace had returned from his travels, he'd changed considerably. He'd visited some of the most romantic cities in the world, and even though he'd experienced good times, his share of romance and a lifetime of culinary inspiration, he'd never been more lonely. For the first time, he wished he could have shared those things with someone special.

That fact had never been as clear as it was tonight. He'd invited his closest friends over, and it wasn't until they'd walked through his door that he'd realized it—they were all couples…and he was single.

Although Garett didn't count. He *was* part a couple, but with a different woman for each occasion.

After returning to his empty apartment, Ace had to face that he was tired of avoiding long-term relationships. But thanks to the memories of his parents' rocky marriage, he still wasn't sure he could make one work.

"At least we'll be able to watch you two on television," Marcel's wife, Simone, said, helping herself to another hors d'oeuvre. She and Marcel were both French Creole from Louisiana. Marcel had joined Ace's staff when the couple had moved to New York after Hurricane Katrina.

"We're going to record every episode on our DVR," Spence said, "so we can watch you win as many times as we want. Who are the other chefs in the competition?"

Putting down his serving tray, Ace sat on the arm on the sofa and looked toward Garett. "I'm not sure."

"Didn't you read the information packet I sent you? Everything you need to know is there."

Ace got up and pulled the thick packet of Gourmet TV paperwork from his desk drawer. He started flipping pages until he saw the list of names of the other competitors. He read them aloud, pausing for a second when he got to the last name. "Veronica Howard."

"Ronnie Howard? Didn't you two go to culinary school together?" Marcel asked.

Ace nodded. During those four years, they'd had a lot of fun together—despite doing their best to one-up each other. He frowned, realizing it had been almost two years since he'd last seen her.

"The good news is," Spence said, "there isn't anyone on that list that you can't take."

"You think so?" he asked, hiding a cocky grin. "What about Etta Foster? She's an icon. In fact, for this show all of my competitors have multiple wins under their belts. It's not going to be a piece of cake."

While his friends debated the strengths and weaknesses of each competitor, Ace went back into the kitchen to check on his braised beef. As he stirred the hearts-of-palm risotto, his mind wandered back to Ronnie.

He wondered what she'd been up to. They'd been close in school, but hadn't spent much time together in the years since then. His career had taken off quickly, sending them in opposite directions. But now Ronnie's career was starting to pick up momentum, setting them back on converging paths.

It would be really good to see her again, he thought, turning off the heat beneath his copper saucepan. Her sassy wit always made him laugh. Hanging out with Ronnie in a great city like Las Vegas or Paris was a good time just waiting to happen.

She was the only woman he'd gotten close to without being romantically involved. Of course, if he'd had his way, they would have hooked up long ago. But Ronnie wasn't having it. She'd always blown off his flirtations with the taunt that she was too much woman for him.

Even though she was full figured, he'd never taken her words literally. Tall, short, thick or thin—he valued variety in women the way he valued variety in fine wine. And Ronnie had voluptuous curves and a pretty face that had always reeled him in.

But she'd also had a jerky boyfriend back then who'd made his skin crawl. In fact, for as long as he'd known her, she'd been in one relationship or another. Last time they'd spoken, she was dating a food critic whom Ace had always despised.

Taking out seven square serving dishes, he began plating his beef and risotto. For all he knew, Ronnie could be married by now, he thought with a grimace.

But, he thought, carrying the first two plates to the dining table, there was always the chance that she was free. If that was the case, anything could happen.

With that flicker of hope, Ace realized he was looking forward to this competition more than ever.

Chapter 2

After a busy night's service at Crave in trendy Georgetown, Ronnie looked over her staff, who'd gathered to see her off.

"Now, you all know the rules. Even though I won't be here in person for a while, you'd better maintain my standards. My spies are everywhere."

Though she pretended to scold them, Ronnie felt deeply grateful for the predominantly female talent she'd been able to assemble for her first restaurant. It was a man's world, and she'd taken a gamble scouring culinary schools for female chefs.

Fortunately, she'd hit the jackpot. Even though they'd been untried, she'd been able to train the eager staff to her satisfaction. Ronnie had confidence in them, even though this would be the longest she'd ever left them on their own.

"Don't worry about a thing," her restaurant manager,

Callie, assured her. The petite blonde was a business dynamo. "All you have to think about is bringing back that hundred-thousand-dollar check."

"We've got it in the bag," said La Quanique Collin-Silverberg, her top sous chef, who would be at her side throughout the competition.

Despite her unconventional name, La Quanique, or LQ as Ronnie liked to call her, was the only person Ronnie trusted in a high-pressure situation because she was genuinely invested in Ronnie's success. Second-generation African and newly converted to Judaism for her husband, she had skin the color of dark espresso, was Amazon tall and wore her hair in a tightly braided updo that sprouted out of her crown like the spikes of a sea urchin.

Her staff took turns cheering the team on with words of encouragement, until one finally interrupted the love fest for an announcement. "We got you a little something for good luck."

Ronnie felt her skin heating. "You didn't have to do anything special for us," she said, in a rare shy moment as Callie gave her and LQ gold lapel pins embossed with Crave's art deco logo.

Ronnie thanked her staff profusely. "These will come in handy. With the competition we'll be facing, we're going to need all the luck we can get."

LQ shook her head, pushing up her square black frame glasses. "We don't need luck. We have everything we need right here," she said, tapping Ronnie's temple.

Ronnie felt her eyes welling up as she took in the confident smiles of her staff. She just hoped she'd be able to live up to their expectations.

On the day of her flight, Ronnie arrived at the airport early. *Check,* she thought, ticking off an item on her mental list. She'd eased one fear in the barrage that made up her flight anxiety—would she miss her plane? Would her baggage arrive on time? Would the plane land safely?

Even though she hated to fly, it was a necessary evil, and she refused to let it get the best of her. But it was a process, and she was still working through it. After clearing security without getting stripped naked or carried off in handcuffs, Ronnie crossed another worry off her list. Now her stomach was making an audible plea for breakfast.

Heading to a coffee shop, she was immediately assaulted by the smell of her favorite treat, a tall whipped-cream-laden mocha latte. The barista put it in the waiting hand of yet another temptation, a tall chocolate-skinned man in an expensive suit.

He saw her looking and nodded. "You should try one. It's delicious."

In a moment of whimsy, she imagined asking the barista for a dark sexy gentleman with a good job and no emotional baggage.

In the real world, Ronnie smiled and shook her head no. In the past she would have ordered that mocha latte, filled it with extra sugar and then drank it alongside a warm, buttery Danish. Today she told the barista, "I'll just have a small black coffee and the fruit cup."

After she received her breakfast, Ronnie perched herself on a stool at a long counter that faced the airport traffic. Seconds later, the sexy guy in the suit parked himself next to her with his latte and Danish.

"Where's your flight headed?" he asked, flashing a flirtatious smile.

Ronnie had to resist the urge to give her answering smile its full wattage. "Las Vegas," she said in a neutral tone.

"What a coincidence. I'm going to Las Vegas for business, too."

Ronnie wanted to bat her eyelashes and sweet-talk him. Handsome and well dressed was just her type. But sweets weren't the only things restricted from her diet these days.

So she just nodded politely, not encouraging further conversation.

"Since we're both going to be in town, maybe we could—"

Ronnie was already shaking her head. "Sorry. I'm going strictly for business, and there just won't be any time to socialize."

Picking up her coffee and fruit cup, she slid off her stool with her heart hammering in her chest. She felt awful, but she had to believe she was doing the right thing. No sweets because they were bad for her health. No men because they were bad for her heart.

Once in a while, she allowed herself to eat something sinful, but Ronnie didn't know when she could trust herself with a man again. Like food, she loved men, and when left to her own devices, she always picked the ones that were bad for her.

Ronnie stumbled off the plane in Las Vegas, feeling rumpled and irritable. It had been a miserable flight, and now all she wanted to do was get her luggage and go.

She made her way to baggage claim, then watched the carousel circle, trying to stay back from the fray of elbowing passengers hauling their bags away.

After several minutes, she spotted her navy-blue bag. Timing her approach carefully, she made a grab for it. But, at that same time, a large man who'd been talking on his cell phone with his back to the carousel spotted the bag and went for it.

The bag slipped from her fingers as he pulled it out of her grasp.

Temper spiking, Ronnie said, "Watch it, man! That's mine. See, I wrote my name on the label in neon-green ink."

"Oh, sorry, ma'am," he said, immediately setting the bag down in front of her.

Ronnie shot a glaring look upward and froze in place. She was staring at none other than The Sexy Chef himself.

Pressing her fingers to her lips in surprise, she said, "Oh my gosh, I can't believe it. Ace Brown."

He flashed his perfect white teeth. "Well, yes. It's always a pleasure to be recognized by a fan."

The smile died from Ronnie's lips. She searched his face to see if this was some sort of joke. Instead she saw a friendly distance in his eyes.

Ronnie had been looking forward to seeing Ace's reaction to her new, slimmer figure, but she doubted she looked *that* different from her former self.

Instead of being flattered, Ronnie found herself getting ticked off. She'd finally come face-to-face with her old friend Ace Brown, and he didn't have a clue who she was.

Chapter 3

Preoccupied, Ace had given the woman before him only a cursory glance. He'd been trying to reach Garett because he couldn't remember if GTV was sending a car, or if he was supposed to take a cab.

Even in that brief look, he'd noted that the woman was attractive, and he was always happy to meet a fan of his show.

Not having any luck reaching his publicist, he tucked his cell phone into the back pocket of his jeans. Ace looked up in time to see the woman's face go from pleasantly surprised to angry.

His brows knit. Why on earth would a perfect stranger be mad—

Then it hit him. She wasn't a perfect stranger. He might not have recognized her right away, but after *really* looking at her face for a few seconds, he began to see those familiar espresso-colored eyes, her juicy plum lips and her pert little nose.

"Oh my God. Ronnie? Is that you?"

Her features were just about the only things that hadn't changed. Somehow his friend had gone from cuddly cutie to buxom bombshell. Her round face was more narrow and her waist more slim, but, thankfully, she still had those voluptuous curves where it counted.

She'd always been attractive, but facts were facts. Now she was hot. He had to force himself to look away before his ogling became cartoonish.

Her lips twitched, but not into the smile he was hoping for. "Oh, so now you recognize me."

He sighed sheepishly. "I'm sorry. I was distracted. It's been a while since I've seen you, and I wasn't expecting to run into you just now. But, you look fantastic and…I'm rambling, aren't I," he said, when her expression remained impassive.

She simply nodded.

Her rumpled clothing and slightly mussed topknot suggested that she'd had a rough flight. But Ace still couldn't stop staring at her. The new Ronnie was a slice of perfection.

Dressed in hip-hugging caramel slacks, a scooped cherry-red tank and a butter-soft leather blazer the color of roasted peanuts, she looked good enough to top a hot fudge sundae. Her form-fitting clothes showed off her feminine curves.

She cleared her throat, and Ace pulled himself together. "I guess we were on the same flight. I should have realized when I made my connection at Dulles, but I didn't see you on the plane."

Ronnie rolled her eyes. "That's because I was in coach."

He frowned, confused. "Didn't the show fly you—"

"Yes, but it's a long story." She picked up the handle on

her rolling luggage and searched for the exit. "I guess I'll see you at the hotel."

Surprised by her dismal mood, Ace stared after her. Was she so upset just because he hadn't recognized her right away? No, it had to be something else. Even though they'd been out of touch for a while, they'd been too close for something so petty to come between them.

Grabbing his luggage off the carousel, Ace headed toward the exit. To his relief, there was a driver outside holding a sign with his name on it. The man led him to a black sedan waiting at the curb and opened the door for him.

He slid across the seat and found a pleasant surprise. Ronnie was already in the car. "And we meet again."

She nodded without her usual enthusiasm, and Ace knew he had to get to the bottom of this once and for all.

"It's a short drive to the hotel. So you'd better talk fast."

She frowned. "What are you talking about?"

"Your long story. What happened on the plane? I can tell it's put you in a bad mood. And Vegas is a party town. I can't let you show up with the wrong attitude."

With a heavy sigh, Ronnie said, "I've always been a nervous flyer, but I was actually looking forward to this trip. But when I boarded the plane and tried to claim my seat in first class, some guy was already sitting there. We called the flight attendant to sort it out. Apparently the flight was overbooked, and we were both given the same seat assignment."

Ace shook his head. "So why didn't the guy move?"

"Because of the age-old rule that applies in these situations."

"What's that?"

"Finders, keepers." From there she described an uncomfortable ride in coach, wedged between a snoring business-man and a mother cradling a cranky newborn. "It might not have been so bad if the guy next to me hadn't passed gas in his sleep during the entire fight."

Ace reached for the complimentary bottle of champagne in the minibar in front of them. "Sounds like we need to put this trip back on the right track, starting with a glass of bubbly."

He popped the cork, filled two flutes halfway and clinked glasses with her. "Here's to a fantastic journey. And to winning."

Ronnie clinked his glass, flashing her eyes at him mischievously. "It's so kind of you to drink to my victory."

Ace grinned, happy to see the sassy girl he knew returning. "Oh? You think you can beat me?"

"I know I can. I've changed a lot more than my dress size since I saw you last."

Not sure if he should broach the subject, Ace couldn't resist asking, "So what *did* make you decide to…get so fit? You always used to say that if you lost weight people would think your food wasn't any good."

"That's another long story. One we don't have time for now. Suffice it to say it was time. Besides, I've finally gotten to the point where my food speaks for itself."

Ace saluted her with his glass. "I heard you opened a restaurant in Georgetown."

"Crave. You should come by next time you're in D.C. I might even give you a professional discount."

"You don't need to give me a discount," he said, teasing. "I'll just pay for my meal out of the prize money when I win."

She cut her eyes to him. "Honey, I don't know if you're aware…but, there is no prize for second place."

Ace threw his head back and laughed. He'd forgotten just how fiercely competitive they'd been in culinary school. Hearing her talk smack the way she used to was arousing his drive to win, among other things.

Winning hadn't been his strongest motivation when he'd agreed to do the competition. He'd been more interested in trying out the new techniques he'd picked up on his European travels. But after five minutes in Ronnie's presence, he suddenly wanted nothing more than to win just for the bragging rights.

"You're so confident *now*," he taunted, "but you may have gotten in over your head. It's not just me you have to beat. You have the culinary queen, Etta Foster, to compete with. Not to mention Ann Le Marche and Stewart Compton. Are a fledgling restaurant and a couple of *Food Fight* wins enough to back up all your big talk?"

Ronnie drained her champagne glass. "Don't you worry about me, Ace. My biggest advantage is that I'm the underdog. Underestimating me will be your downfall."

Ace knew first hand not to underestimate Veronica Howard. She'd always been tenacious and eager to learn. He had no doubt that she would be good competition. But his reputation spoke for itself.

"I just want to make sure you haven't forgotten just how things went down in culinary school. Soufflés, marinades, knife skill—I got better grades in all those areas. Plus, I've been honing my craft with some of the masters around Europe." He popped the collar on his polo shirt. "You don't want none of this."

"And? I got better grades in pastry and desserts," Ronnie said, waving him off. "Plus, I've got a lot of new tricks up my sleeves. And your chef's jacket doesn't even *have* sleeves."

Caught off guard, Ace laughed. When he'd started doing

his show, *The Sexy Chef,* it had been Garett's idea to take the sleeves off his jacket.

"Europe or no Europe," Ronnie continued. "I've seen what you do, and I'm ready to take you *and* the others on. We'll prove ourselves in the kitchen soon enough. But for now I just want to salvage what's left of this day and enjoy being in Las Vegas."

With their obligatory trash talk out of the way, Ace swiveled in his seat, letting his knee touch hers. *Damn she looked good,* he thought, resisting the urge to say it out loud.

Was she single? No ring on her finger. He hoped she wasn't still dating that jerky food critic.

Unable to ask what he really wanted to know, he asked instead, "Is this your first time in Las Vegas?"

"Yes, I was supposed to come for a bachelorette party once, but I got the flu and had to stay home. The girls told me all about the fun I'd missed. Gambling, Chippendale dancers, staying up all night—"

"So much for What happens in Vegas stays in Vegas."

She sighed. "I know. I'm still mad that I couldn't go."

"Then you'll just have to make up for it this time. I don't know how much you'll be able to squeeze in, but there's the rest of today and part of tomorrow."

"There are three things I want to accomplish before I leave Vegas. First, I want to gamble in the casino—not just slot machines like I've played in Atlantic City—but some real table gambling. Then I want to see a show. I love Cirque du Soleil."

"And the last thing?"

"I just want to perform well enough to make it to round two," she said, showing vulnerability for the first time as she rested her forehead in her palm. "Ugh, I don't want to be the first to go home."

"That doesn't seem like too much to ask for."

Ace smiled, both happy to be with his old friend again and excited by the crackling tension he felt between them. Was it mutual this time?

It could be. Her eyes had taken on a coy slant as she lowered her lashes to hide her normally direct gaze. When she raised them again, he saw her eyes trace his body from where their knees touched slowly up his frame.

Time to make his move. "Ronnie, are you—"

Before he could ask if she was seeing anyone, the car stopped. They had arrived at The Venetian hotel, where the first leg of the *All-Star Food Fight* would take place. The chauffeur pulled open their door just as things were getting interesting.

Bellhops instantly appeared, and the two of them were ushered off to check in. Unfortunately, Ace didn't get the opportunity to finish his question.

On the elevator ride to his room, he made a silent vow.

If they were both as good as they thought they were in the kitchen, they would have up to three weeks together on the road. Ace decided it was finally time for him to take a shot at romancing the chef.

Chapter 4

The bellhop let Ronnie into her luxury concierge suite. As soon as she saw the giant, king-size bed, a huge smile spread across her face.

Thankfully Ace had helped her dispel the gloomy mood that had developed during the flight. Now her arrival at the hotel pushed her back into full elation.

After quickly unpacking her clothes, she walked over to the window to discover she had a fantastic view of the gigantic pool. Instantly, Ronnie craved a swim in the cool water.

Even though she had to run down to the event gallery to make sure the boxes she'd shipped had arrived, there were two motivating factors calling her to the pool. One was the hot Las Vegas sun, and two was the promise she'd made to Cara that she'd work out regularly while she was away.

After confirming that her shipment had arrived safely,

Ronnie changed into her bathing suit and headed out to the pool. But old habits died hard, and she covered her suit with a T-shirt and shorts as well as a long terrycloth robe.

Grabbing some towels, Ronnie set herself up in a lounge chair. The water was calling to her, but on such a hot afternoon, the pool was packed. Even though she'd lost a lot of weight since the last time she'd been swimming in a public pool, she still couldn't bring herself to undress.

"Wow. I'm getting hot just looking at you."

Ronnie looked up and found Ace standing over her. She silently caught her breath. A towel was slung around his neck and his chest was bare, showing every bulging muscle, from his abs to his pecs and biceps. His red swim trunks were wet and clung to his large, muscular thighs. Ronnie had to school her eyes to stay away from his lower body.

But there was no safe place for her eyes to rest when there were big muscles and sleek brown skin everywhere she tried to look.

"Ace. I guess we had the same idea about how to spend the rest of our afternoon."

He laughed. "I don't know about you, but I was actually *swimming* in the pool. Did you forget you're in the desert? Because you're better dressed for the Alaskan tundra."

Feeling embarrassed, Ronnie shook her head. "No, I just got here. I'm planning to get in." A bead of perspiration slid down between her breasts under all her layers of clothing.

"Well, come on. Take off your snow suit and get in with me."

Ronnie's skin became even hotter under Ace's watchful gaze. It was one thing to show off her new figure under a carefully chosen outfit that complimented her shape. If she undressed now, there would be nothing left to the imagination.

"You go ahead. I'll be there in a minute."

He shook his head. "What are you waiting for? Come on in. The water is perfect. I know you're roasting under that robe."

Ronnie realized that if she protested any further she'd sound foolish, so she bit her lip and stood up. Untying her robe, she slipped it off and took her time folding it on her lounge chair.

Ace immediately snickered. "I can't believe you have even more clothes on under that robe."

Swallowing hard, Ronnie took off her shorts first, letting the length of her T-shirt cover her suit. Suddenly, she was overwhelmed with nerves. Even though her mirror showed her a thin person when she looked in it, she still felt like an overweight person on the inside. She'd always made a big show of confidence and bravado when it had come to her body in the past.

But now that Ace was standing there waiting for her to disrobe, all that confidence eluded her. All she could imagine was the disappointment in his face when he saw her in her modest black tank suit.

Trying to come up with some witty distraction to hide her insecurities, Ronnie whipped her T-shirt over her head like a child ripping off a bandage.

But her witty remark died on her lips as her gaze raised to Ace's. Before she could utter a sound, he said, "Very sexy."

Then she was scooped up in his arms and summarily dumped into the swimming pool.

When she came up sputtering water, the tension of the moment had been broken. Ace was suddenly next to her splashing water in her direction.

"You were moving too slow. I didn't have the patience to watch you dip one toe, then the other before you declared the water too cold. So I thought I'd help you along. You're welcome."

"You—" Without thinking, Ronnie jumped on his back and pushed his head under the water.

Ace burst to the surface, laughing. He quickly grabbed her around the waist and held her so she couldn't get at him again.

As her own laughter began to subside, she began to realize that only a thin, wet layer of bathing suit separated her bare skin from his. Feeling her self-consciousness returning, Ronnie began to kick her feet and flail her arms, sending wave after wave of water at Ace until he dumped her back into the water.

She felt safer, hidden under the surface of the water. "I'm free," she said, goading him to chase her.

They played a cat-and-mouse game around the pool, carefully dodging the other occupants. Ronnie was able to evade Ace's grasp for quite some time, until she made the mistake of feinting left when she should have feinted right.

"I've got you now," he shouted, as she found herself locked in his arms.

Before she could stop herself, she said, "And just what are you going to do with me now that you've got me?"

"Whatever I want, of course." His tone was light and playful, but she could see heat rising in his eyes.

Suddenly it was more than Ronnie was prepared to handle. She didn't come to Las Vegas to have an affair. Especially not with the ridiculously hot Sexy Chef.

Immediately Ronnie began squirming in his arms. But that only made the situation worse. Ronnie applied a little pressure against his muscular embrace and quickly realized there was no escape. Ace's arms were like bands of steel holding her against him. And her struggles caused an exciting friction between their bodies. Suddenly the heat in his eyes wasn't the only thing rising.

Clearly a bit startled himself, his grip on her loosened and Ronnie wriggled free. In a full panic now, she dove under the surface and swam to the nearest ladder. She didn't care that she had to now walk halfway around the pool to get back to her things.

Barely taking the time to fully cover herself, she gathered up her clothes and started heading for the hotel entrance.

"Ronnie!" Ace called out from somewhere behind her.

Darting a quick look over her shoulder, she waved in his general direction. "I'm going to go back inside," she called to him. "I'll see you later."

Ace stood on the pool deck, watching Ronnie literally run away from him. Granted, things had progressed faster than he'd intended, but he hadn't expected this kind of reaction from her.

Ronnie had always been sassy and confident. Ace couldn't quite wrap his mind around it, but it seemed that since Ronnie had lost weight, she had become self-conscious.

It was obvious in the way that she'd dressed for the pool in layer after layer of clothing. It had seemed as though she was avoiding disrobing in front of him. From the way she'd been acting, he'd half expected to see gruesome burn scars or massive stretch marks, but her body had been tight and toned. The only thing wrong with her shape had been that matronly tank suit that covered up too much of it.

He'd wanted to stare, openly admiring her new figure, but, on impulse, he'd decided to drop her into the pool. He'd gotten the desired reaction. She'd been too angry to focus on her hang-ups…at least at first.

If only he'd been able to keep his hands off her, she might not have run from him. But that only made him more determined than ever to let her know how he'd been feeling about her.

"There you are. I've been looking all over this place for you," Ace heard Garett say, walking toward him, looking like a fifties throwback in his straw fedora, white cabana shirt and pale plaid pants.

"Get a load of you, Frank Sinatra," Ace said, looking his publicist up and down.

"Hey, if you think I'm not going to make the most of my time in Vegas, you're crazy."

"And here I thought you traveled all this way to give me moral support."

"Why don't you dry off and come inside, Ace. We have work to do. The press junket is tomorrow, and I want to do a little prep."

Ace started across the pool deck to the lounge chair where he'd left his things. "I do press all the time. I really don't think I need to prep."

What he really wanted to do was go after Ronnie. He had a feeling that the more time he gave her, the more she'd be able to convince herself that nothing had happened between them.

"Of course we have to prep," Garett said, coming up behind him. "We need an angle. Something that will make you stand out from the other contestants."

Ace shrugged, drying himself off with his towel. "I'll stand out from the others when I win."

"We can't wait until then. We need to find an angle now. Something that will make them follow you for the entire competition."

Ace pulled his on T-shirt over his head. He should have been used to Garett's push for publicity stunts by now.

Instead, he chose to ignore him most of the time. And it wasn't lost on his friend that Ace was distracted at the moment.

"You're not focused. Does this have anything to do with the girl I saw hurrying away from you just now?"

"She's not just some girl. That's Ronnie." At his friend's blank expression, Ace continued. "You know, Veronica Howard. She's in the competition."

"Are you kidding me? I didn't even recognize her." Garett rubbed his chin. "I don't know how I feel about you mingling with your competitors. Unless, of course, you were trying to get in her head. Psych her out a bit?"

Ace waved him off. "We have a healthy rivalry going, but I'm not trying to get in her head. Ronnie and I are friends."

Garett studied him for a minute, nodding his head. "I get it. Not in her head, just in her pants."

Ace was so taken aback, he didn't deny it. He just gaped at Garett.

He snapped his fingers. "Yeah, that's perfect. We've found our angle."

"What are you talking about?" Ace asked, stepping into his flip-flops.

"I'm talking about the 'showmance,' my friend. The classic reality-TV romance. We let it leak that there may be a little more than competition heating up between you and your competitor, Ms. Veronica Howard. The press will eat it up. They'll be jumping out of trash cans to catch you two sneaking around together."

"Hold on, Garett, that's the last thing I want. You'd better go back to the drawing board, because that angle's not going to work."

Garett slung an arm around Ace's shoulder as they

headed inside the hotel. "So you're denying that you're interested in her?"

"No," Ace said, twisting out from under his friend's arm. "But my interest in her has nothing to do with manufacturing a 'showmance' for the sake of the press."

"Look, if you're going to pursue her anyway, why not kill two birds with one stone? Let your little fling work to our advantage?"

"It's not going to happen, Garett. That's final."

Once Ronnie was safe in her hotel room, she breathed a sigh of relief. Had she and Ace really been flirting with each other?

Never in a million years had she imagined that he could actually see her that way. Of course, circumstances were different now. She'd lost a lot of weight. Now she was finally in the ballpark of being his type.

She didn't know why, but that thought bothered her quite a bit. It was understandable that wearing a smaller size would make her more attractive to a wider pool of men. But she secretly wished she'd been his type *before* she'd lost the weight.

Ronnie hopped into the shower and washed and dried her hair. When she came out of the bathroom, her mind was still whirling with the memory of what had happened at the pool.

What she needed now was a bit of perspective. Picking up her cell phone, she dialed Cara.

"Hello?"

"Greetings from Vegas, baby!"

"Ronnie. You made it." Her friend's voice sounded far away. "If you're calling to check up on Baxter, relax. He's having the time of his life playing with the kids."

"I'm so glad. But I miss my little puppy." At eighty

pounds, her German shepherd was well into adulthood, but Baxter would always be a puppy to Ronnie.

"He misses you, too," Cara said and Ronnie heard an echo in the background.

"Do you have me on speakerphone?"

"Yes, I'm in the car. I'm on my way to pick up the kids from day care. A.J.'s working late today."

"Then I won't keep you. You can call me back later."

"Wait a minute. I know you didn't call just to say hello and good-bye. What's on your mind?"

"I think I'm in trouble," Ronnie said, sinking down on the edge of her bed.

"Oh, no. What kind of trouble?"

"The usual. Man trouble."

"You haven't been in Las Vegas for even twenty-four hours and you already have man trouble…. Good for you!"

"I'm glad you think this is funny."

"It's not funny. It's great. Who's the guy?"

"Ace Brown." Ronnie flopped onto her back, staring up at the ceiling. She felt like a high school girl with a crush. It was embarrassing.

"I should have known. He caught sight of your new hot bod and couldn't resist you."

Ronnie sighed. "Something like that."

"Then what's the problem? You two have been friends for years. He's a good guy. You like him. He's gorgeous. Sounds like a win/win to me."

"Yeah, but he's always been a player. And he never showed any interest in me when I was…pleasantly plump."

"Ahh, I see. I guess I can understand why that would bother you. But, you've got to get over it. Tell me exactly what happened."

"Well, I ran into him at the airport, and he didn't even recognize me. I mean I know I've lost weight, but do I really look that different?"

"No, but you have to give him the benefit of the doubt. It was probably a context thing. You probably caught him off guard. He didn't know how much you've changed. What happened after that?"

Ronnie told her friend about the ride to the hotel and running into Ace at the pool.

"Ooh, steamy. Well, he's clearly into you. You might have actually gotten somewhere with him if you hadn't run away."

"You're not helping me at all here, Cara."

"What? Because I'm not encouraging you to continue your forced celibacy? No one was happier than me when you finally got Andre out of your life. But you can't keep punishing yourself for that mistake."

Sure, if her on-and-off relationship with Andre Roberts had been her only mistake, maybe she could get past it. But every guy she'd dated since high school had treated her poorly. For the longest time she thought that was just how relationships were. And then her best friend found her own soulmate in A. J. Gray, and Ronnie began to realize she deserved more.

"He wasn't the first. I have a pattern of picking guys like Andre. How am I ever supposed to trust my own judgment again?"

"Now that your eyes are wide-open, you'll never let a man take advantage of you like that again. Ronnie, believe me, it's time to get back in the game."

She shook her head at the phone. "No, this isn't the right time. Maybe after the competition is over—"

"There's no time like the present. If you wait until after the competition…well, for one thing, Ace might not be around. And you'll just find another excuse to put this off."

"But I need to stay focused."

"Listen. You're going to win the competition. But that doesn't mean you can't reacquaint yourself with an old friend at the same time. Just go out with him. Have fun. It doesn't have to be a lifetime commitment."

Finally, Ronnie sighed, giving up. "You've got a one-track mind, and that track leads to Ace."

"Why did you call if you didn't want my opinion?"

"Fine. You win. If he asks me out, and that's a big if, I won't say no."

"That's all I can ask for. Okay, I just pulled up to the school. Gotta go. But keep me updated, okay?"

"You've got it. But if this turns out to be a big mistake, I'm not going to miss my chance to say I told you so."

Chapter 5

After Cara's pep talk, Ronnie remembered that she'd wanted this trip to Las Vegas to be fun. She'd promised her best friend that she'd jump back into the dating world, and she knew she'd have to keep that promise eventually, but something was still holding her back.

She wanted to dress up and hit the Strip, but instead she stayed in her hotel room, watching rental movies and ordering from room service. It was a tame, restful evening, and when she woke up the next morning, Ronnie felt like a coward.

She washed her face and stared at her reflection in the mirror. Sometimes it still shocked her to see that her face was no longer perfectly round. It had narrowed, revealing high cheekbones and a defined chin. The transformation moved her on the beauty spectrum, further away from cute and closer to beautiful.

Before, she would embrace her heavier stature and had defied anyone to tell her she wasn't amazing in every way.

Strangely enough, now that she was thin, she'd lost her wall of defense. She constantly felt vulnerable and exposed. She missed sassy, confident Ronnie. But today was a new day. It was time to own the changes she'd made in her life and to stop hiding.

And she couldn't ask for better timing. Today she had a press junket that would take most of the day. What better chance to show the world that she knew what she wanted and planned to take it.

LQ would be arriving in the evening to help her plot out a strategy for whatever GTV would spring on them tomorrow. Maybe she'd be able to convince her sous chef to hit the town with her. She had big plans for her last free night in Vegas.

But before that, she was going to be trapped in a room with reporters. There was also a photo shoot, during which they'd take promotion shots of each chef in their jackets. That meant Ronnie had to take special care with her appearance that morning. Her chef's jacket was tinged pink because Ronnie thought typical white chefs' coats were boring, and she was anything but.

Setting her hair in hot rollers, she took a steamy hot shower, then carefully applied her makeup. A little raspberry lipstick for her full lips and just a hint of sparkling charcoal-gray at her eyes to make them pop. Finally she smoothed her dark curls into gentle waves that framed her face. It was a bit more glamour than she usually wore in the kitchen, but she had to look her best for the photos.

The extra effort wasn't for Ace, she told herself. But if he happened to notice, it couldn't hurt. Unfortunately, as she slipped on her chef's jacket and hustled toward the elevator, Ronnie realized that all that extra attention to her appearance had made her slightly late.

She showed up at the hotel ballroom at the tail end of

the buffet breakfast that GTV had provided. Of course, Ace was the first person she saw as she entered the room.

"There you are. I was starting to wonder if you were going to make it," he said, refilling his coffee cup.

It didn't help matters that he looked delicious. His sleeveless chef's jacket might have been a bit self-indulgent, but as Ronnie took in those giant biceps, she couldn't help wondering what sleeves *could* contain them.

"Better late than never," Ronnie said, filling a small bowl with fruit and pouring herself a cup of black coffee. The cheese Danish was whispering, *Ronnie, Ronnie*, in her ear, but she made it through another breakfast without giving in.

Nodding good-bye to Ace, Ronnie took her food and crossed the room to take a seat. She couldn't risk standing there making awkward conversation. It wouldn't have been long before he'd brought up yesterday's embarrassingly hasty exit. Yes, she had literally run away from him, she thought with a private wince.

Taking a long sip of her coffee, she sat down next to Stewart Compton. Rail thin, with shoulder-length blond hair and a long hooked nose, Stewart was the most flamboyant of the bunch.

Even though they'd never competed against each other, Ronnie had seen him backstage at several studio tapings. He always made bold choices with his food, so it would be interesting to see what he came up with tomorrow.

He looked her up and down before a wide smile broke out on his face. "Check you out, Ms. Thang. You look fabulous."

"Thank you, darling. You're not so bad yourself," she said, admiring his crisp white chef's jacket with navy-and-gold piping on the collar and sleeves. His restaurant logo looked like a family crest with the words Compton Arms stitched below it.

He leaned close to whisper in her ear. "You don't know how glad I am to see your friendly face, sweetie. Everyone in here has their game face on. Especially her," Stewart said, glaring in Ann Le Marche's direction.

In the kitchen, Ann was all business, so it wasn't surprising that she had no appreciation for Stewart's fun-loving, gossipy nature. Whereas Stewart's food was whimsical and bright, hers was sparse and symmetrical.

Ronnie picked up a handful of berries. "I know, I could feel the tension the second I walked in here. I guess the promise of such a huge check has everyone on edge."

"Honey, if Ann was any edgier, she wouldn't need a stone to sharpen her knives."

Ronnie laughed, realizing that Stewart was referring to Ann's style as well as her demeanor. She wore heavy black-rimmed glasses and blood-red lipstick, and her spiky hair was bleached to a shocking platinum blond. Her elaborate tattoos peeked out along the neck and wrists of her black Nehru jacket.

"Ann's tough competition," Ronnie whispered back to Stewart. "But I'm most worried about *her,*" she said, nodding toward Etta Foster, who was quietly nibbling the corners of a homemade muffin while crocheting an afghan.

"Ahh, the grand dame herself." Stewart nodded. "She's a veritable culinary mogul. We should be honored just to breathe the same air she does."

Etta had always reminded Ronnie of Betty White with her blonde/white hair curling around her ears and the broad, wholesome smile that puffed out her cheeks. She wore the whitest chef's jacket of everyone, fitted perfectly at the waist with matching pants. Even her logo stitched on the breast of her jacket was white.

Just then, the director came in to give them an overview of how the following weeks would go, and Ronnie had just enough time to gobble down a handful of berries and drain her coffee cup.

After the orientation, all of the chefs were led into a connecting room with tables set up around the perimeter. Ronnie tried not to feel self-conscious as she took in the displays of promotional items filling the tables of the other chefs. Most of them, like Ace, had a line of cookbooks to show off. And Etta Foster's table was so full her tiny face could barely be seen among the stacks of cookbooks, cookware and other merchandise.

Ronnie took a seat at her table. She didn't have a publicist, so she'd had to produce her own promotional item. It was a cardboard foldout of her standing in front of Crave on the right, and her restaurant menu on the left.

It didn't take up as much space as a tower of cookbooks, but she was proud of the glossy piece that showed off her dream-come-true. As she looked out over the room, Ronnie was smacked with the reality of just how big this competition was going to be.

Normally these press gatherings were small, with just a few reporters from the local area looking for human interest pieces. This time, though, the press had more than tripled in number, and they represented all the major news outlets and food publications across the country.

As the press began circulating, Ronnie warmed to it quickly. Sometimes it could get tedious answering the same questions over and over, but Ronnie didn't mind this time. She had fun joking with the reporters and finding new ways to respond to similar questions.

"You've got some heavy-hitting competition in this

All-Star Food Fight. Does that intimidate you at all?" a journalist from *Food and Wine* magazine asked.

"You said it yourself, it's *all*-star. That makes me a star, too, and I plan to blind them with my shine."

Bon Appétit magazine asked, "Would you consider yourself an underdog going into the first round tomorrow?"

"I'm undefeated, just like the other chefs in this competition. All being an underdog means is that no one will be disappointed if I lose. I think that's a great starting position."

Ronnie was having such a good time, she was caught completely off guard when a food critic from her past sat down in front of her.

"Veronica Howard. If I didn't have your name written right in front of me, I wouldn't have believed it was you."

Her temper spiked, bringing a full flush of angry heat to her cheeks. "Andre Roberts. If I hadn't gotten you fired for that libelous review you wrote about me, I wouldn't be so shocked to see you here."

He was her ex-boyfriend, and Ronnie couldn't believe how quickly her day had turned from sweet cream to sour milk.

"Oh, no hard feelings about that, Ronnie. I know we're both adult enough to put all that unpleasantness behind us. Obviously, we've both landed on our feet. Leaving the newspaper turned out to be a good move for me."

Ronnie's eye twitched at his gall. He always found a way to sell his crap as fertilizer.

"Now I've got this sweet gig at *Food Trends* magazine," he continued. "The only downside is that I have to cover cheesy contests like this. But the travel makes it worth it."

Ronnie stared, unblinking, wondering what she'd ever

seen in this jerk. Sure, he was pretty-boy handsome with light skin and gold eyes. He'd chemically processed his hair so it waved against his scalp, and he wore two obnoxious diamond earrings that flaunted money he didn't have.

His looks, like his personality, no longer appealed to her. He was supposed to be interviewing her, but of course all he'd done was talk about himself. And now she could see how he'd used backhanded compliments to keep her down. When they'd dated, he'd had her convinced no other man could want her.

What a fool she'd been.

"I'm sure *Food Trends* isn't paying you to talk about yourself, Andre. So let me help you earn that sweet paycheck. Those gaudy diamonds can't pay for themselves, after all." Before he could respond, she continued. "Yes, I'm an underdog, but I think that works in my favor. No, I'm not intimidated by my competitors. I, too, am undefeated, and I still have a few tricks no one has seen."

As Ronnie talked, Andre grinned at her, making no move to turn on his tape recorder or jot a note down on his pad. "Come on, do you really think you have a shot at winning this thing? I mean, Etta Foster is a legend all by herself."

Ronnie swallowed hard, urging her inner self to remain calm. "Of course I think I have a shot, that's the only reason I'm here—to win. I wouldn't have been invited to compete if I wasn't one of the best."

Andre's brows rose. Clearly he was surprised by the change in her attitude. At that point, he went ahead and asked her a couple of real questions for his magazine.

Relieved that it was almost over, Ronnie answered confidently, pleased to be able to brag a little about her recent success.

"And how does your weight loss factor into your new-found success? Do you think you're a better chef now that you're thin?"

Ronnie felt like she'd been kicked in the gut. She opened her lips to speak, but no words came out. If she could have found anything heavy enough within reach, she would have clobbered him over the head. Instead, all she did was seethe in silence, shooting flames from her eyes.

Laughing, Andre held up a hand. "You don't have to answer that last one."

Hearing his laughter, Ronnie realized she'd given him exactly what he'd wanted. He'd thrown her off her game and made her lose her confidence. That had been his goal all along.

"I've got to move on, but maybe we can catch up later. I'll be in town until tomorrow evening."

Before Ronnie could protest, he walked away, leaving her angry and flustered as the next reporter sat down in his place.

That evening, Ronnie stood in front of her closet. She didn't want to think about seeing her ex-boyfriend or the press conference she'd stumbled through afterward. Tonight she just wanted to get a taste of Vegas and have fun.

She'd promised Cara that she'd give Ace a chance, but she hadn't seen much of him that day. And since he'd always been smooth with the ladies, there was a chance he'd already found company for the evening. But that didn't mean she had to spend another night in her room.

Instead, she pulled out a vibrant green party dress she hadn't yet dared to wear. It was simple in design with spaghetti straps and an A-line silhouette. It fell smoothly over her curves, and the hemline was a lot shorter than anything she normally wore. Yet, it was modest compared to some of the outfits she'd seen the girls in this town wearing.

After slipping into her dress, Ronnie turned her attention to her hair. Outside of work, she loved to be more daring with her styles. She'd become slightly more conservative in the last few years, opting out of the big showy hairdos she'd sported in the past. But she still thought hair was the best way to express her mood.

For tonight, she flat-ironed it straight and sleek, then pulled it back from her face. She added a little extra hair for a long ponytail that would hang to the middle of her back. Ronnie usually went with her own naturally long hair, but this was a special occasion. And sometimes a girl deserved a little extra body.

As soon as Ronnie stepped outside her room, it hit her that she'd be on her own for the night. It seemed a tad sad to be all alone in a party town. Resisting the urge to go back and hide in her room, she headed down to the casino. Despite feeling nervous, she registered for a seat at one of the poker tables. After playing Texas Hold 'Em a few times with her busboys after hours, she felt she might have a chance at holding her own. But several losing rounds quickly sent her back to the familiarity of the slot machines.

Ace found her there twenty minutes later, playing down the last of the twenty-dollar bill she'd fed the machine.

"Hey, big spender," he joked when he saw her playing a nickel machine.

Feeling her heart start to race, Ronnie spun around on her stool. "Hey, Ace."

He grinned at her. "Look at you. You look fantastic."

"Thank you," she said, trying to play off her blush. "I can't help it. It comes naturally."

He nodded in agreement, and Ronnie basked in the pleasure of the genuine attraction in his eyes.

"What are you doing tonight?"

Ronnie's heartbeat thundered. Here it is. He was going to ask her out.

"Nothing much. I was just sitting here killing time—"

Ace opened his mouth to speak, but couldn't utter a sound before a slick gentleman in an expensive suit clapped him on the back. "Ready for dinner, buddy?"

"Yeah, in a minute. Ronnie, this is my publicist, Garett Fontaine. Garett, this is my old friend from culinary school, Veronica Howard."

They shook hands and exchanged greetings, then Ace said, "We're going to have dinner at the hotel's steakhouse. If you don't have plans, why don't you join us?"

As her mouth began to water, Ronnie felt a moment of panic. Steak. She'd like nothing better than to indulge in a thick, juicy prime rib. It was her favorite cut of beef. But she'd already eaten a bland little salad in her room. The salad hadn't done much to fill her stomach, so there was plenty of room left for steak. But if she wanted to keep wearing dresses like the one she had on, she couldn't eat whatever she wanted anymore.

But she didn't want to tell these two handsome men that she couldn't join them because she didn't want to get fat again.

"No, thanks. I'm meeting friends in the V Bar in a few minutes."

Ace frowned. "I didn't know you had friends in town."

"Oh, they're just some people I met earlier. They asked me to hang out with them tonight."

Ace shook his head. "You don't want to spend the evening with strangers. Let two friendly gentlemen treat you to a great meal."

Garett nodded eagerly. "You should definitely join us. It'll give the two of you a chance to catch up. Once the competition starts you become the enemy," he joked.

"That settles it, then, right?"

Ronnie almost gave in. She did promise Cara that she'd go out with Ace if he asked. And lo and behold, he was asking.

Then she pictured herself at the table eating a carrot with a knife and fork while they cut into tender hunks of meat. No, if she went to dinner, she'd get a steak. That meant only one thing.

"Thanks for the invitation. But it really is time for me to get going. Besides, two handsome bachelors like yourselves will have a much better time this evening without me tagging along."

Ronnie cashed out the $2.45 left in the machine, stuffed the claim ticket in her purse and stood. "Maybe I'll run into you guys later."

Ace stared after Ronnie, not believing for a minute that she really had plans for the evening. She was definitely running scared, and he didn't know how he was going to get past her brick walls.

"Sorry, man, I tried to help your cause. Better luck next time." Garett took his arm, dragging him forward. "Let's eat. I'm in the mood for a porterhouse."

Ace walked beside him, ignoring Garett's chatter about the female "talent" he'd spotted during the day. He was still trying to figure out a way through Ronnie's defenses. He'd wanted to make his move tonight. Garett had been right about one thing, though. Once the competition started, she became the opposition.

And as much as he liked her, he still planned to win.

After dinner, Garett wanted to hit the casino, but Ace was tempted to stop by Ronnie's room instead. If her plans were as phony as he suspected, he'd find her there.

"Come on, Ace. You can't leave me hanging like this," Garett said as they left the restaurant.

"You seem to be forgetting that we're here for work, not to party. I have to compete tomorrow, as you keep reminding me."

"Fine, let's compromise. Let me buy you a drink at V Bar. That'll give me some time to find a new companion for the evening. And you won't have to feel guilty about abandoning your best friend."

"You're right. How would I ever have gotten to sleep tonight," Ace said, sarcastically.

They entered the bar and Garett punched him in the arm. "Don't worry about it, buddy. That's why I'm here. To save you from yourself." Then he broke his stride, pausing to stare at a table in the back of the room.

Ace didn't even turn his head. No matter what his friend said, when Garett was on the prowl, he didn't need any help from Ace.

"Hey, isn't that your friend Veronica?"

"What?" Ace swiveled his neck so fast he could have given himself whiplash.

Sure enough, Ronnie was sitting at a table with a rowdy group of girls. One was wearing a short white veil and bending over the table, arms behind her back, to upend a shot using only her mouth. Ronnie and the others were cheering her on.

Surprised, Ace stared in her direction. She must have felt the heat of his gaze because she looked up and caught his eye. Smiling wide, she waved and reluctantly Ace waved back.

He'd been wrong. It seemed she *did* have plans all along.

Feeling a little less sure of himself, he followed Garett to the bar. "I guess I will join you in the casino tonight, Garett. This is Las Vegas, after all."

Ronnie smiled to herself as she watched Ace walk to the bar. He had the perfect butt. Firm, tight, and it filled out his pants beautifully.

Then she blinked in the direction of her thoughts. Sitting up straight, she realized she'd had too many champagne cocktails. She'd had only two, but Ronnie didn't drink much anymore. History had proven that drinking made her... amorous.

One of the girls let out a whoop, bringing Ronnie's attention back to the table. "Okay, we can cross 'get a stranger to buy you a drink' off the list," a tiny blonde said. "We have to leave the bar now and get Jen a body piercing."

Two hours ago, Ronnie had walked into the bar alone, petrified of appearing lonely and desperate. She'd found a table in the back and stared at the drink menu. When she'd been on the verge of creeping back to her room, the bachelorette party had clamored in and swept her up in their celebration.

The girls had a long list of tasks for the bride to complete, and they wanted to borrow Ronnie's lipstick so the bride could kiss the top of a bald man's head. After finding out that Ronnie was on her own for the evening, they'd insisted she join them.

"Wait a minute," one of the girls shouted. "We can't leave until we have another round. Screaming Orgasms for everyone."

* * *

Sometime after midnight, the bachelorette party broke up, and Ronnie found herself teetering toward the hotel elevators with her shoes in her hands.

Still off kilter, Ronnie careened into the side of a man who was already waiting for the elevator.

"Whoa, are you okay, Ronnie?" he said, steadying her on her feet.

"Ace, all I have to do is think about you and you appear." Right now he looked like a giant hot fudge sundae to her and Ronnie knew she was grinning widely at him.

"Sounds like you had a lot of fun with your new friends. You didn't mention that you couldn't join us for dinner because you were attending a bachelorette party."

"Oh, I lied about having plans," Ronnie said, a bit more loose lipped than she had expected. "I met those girls after I got to the bar."

The doors to the elevator opened and Ronnie carefully made her way inside. Ace followed her, laughing under his breath. "I knew it."

Ronnie moved closer to him. "What about you? Did you have fun tonight?"

"It wasn't bad. Obviously I didn't have as much fun as you did. What kind of trouble did you girls get into?"

"Trouble? No trouble." Then a slow grin broke out on her face. "Well, maybe a little."

"That's what I thought."

The elevator chimed and the doors opened on Ronnie's floor. "Aww, our ride is over already."

Ace took her arm and helped her through the doors.

"Ooh, are you on this floor, too?"

"No, but I think I'd better make sure you make it back to your room safely."

She nudged him with her elbow. "What a gentleman," she

said as they stopped in front of her door. "But if you're not too much of a gentleman, you can come in for a while."

He stared at her for a long moment, and Ronnie knew he wanted to say yes.

"That's the best offer I've had all night, but I think we should save that for a time when you're a little less tipsy."

"Then how about a kiss good-night?" Ronnie dropped her purse and shoes on the carpet and pressed herself against him, throwing her arms around his neck.

Their mouths came together in a steamy lip-lock. Ronnie felt like her whole body was floating as she felt the roughness of his light stubble brush against her face.

After a moment, Ace pulled away, setting her back on her feet. Immediately, her foot connected with something round, which rolled under her toes and then started vibrating. "What the—"

With a burst of laughter, Ace reached down. "Looks like you dropped something," he said, handing her the mini-vibrator she'd gotten as a party favor from the bachelorette blowout.

Ronnie giggled, the alcohol in her system taking away her embarrassment. "Oops! I forgot about that."

Ace raised his eyebrows in mock surprise. "I see…."

She dropped it back in her clutch and snapped it shut. "No, you don't, silly. That isn't mine."

"Really? Because it seems to have fallen out of your purse."

"I mean, I didn't buy it. It was a gift. From the party."

"I see." He laughed.

"But, hey, it's just plastic. I prefer the real thing," she said, looking him up and down.

Ace laughed. "Oh, Ronnie, if I thought for a minute you'd feel the same way tomorrow, I'd make good on that suggestion. As it is, I have a feeling you're going to need all the sleep you can get."

He took her purse and found her key card inside. After unlocking her door, he saw her safely inside and then disappeared back into the corridor.

As Ronnie fell back on her bed, her head was spinning. She wasn't sure if it was from the drink or Ace's lips. His face was the last image that floated in her mind as she fell asleep.

Chapter 6

Ronnie woke the next morning with her brain slam-dancing inside her skull. Moaning, she fought to turn off the alarm. Without it, Ronnie wasn't sure she would have awakened before nightfall.

Her eyelids were swollen and the crack of sunlight that made it through the curtains hurt her skewed vision. Clutching her head, she realized this was exactly why she didn't drink.

Swinging her legs off the bed, Ronnie suddenly became aware of a stinging pain coming from her middle. Sending a hand to her abdomen, her fingers ran over something chunky.

Startled, she raced to the bathroom and hiked up the old T-shirt she'd slept in. A simple gold stud was jutting through her navel.

"Oh, no," she moaned, sinking down on the toilet seat before her legs gave out. She hadn't thought she'd had *that* much to drink. But, she now remembered that the bride hadn't wanted to get a piercing unless everyone in the party joined in. Ronnie had tentatively considered a third earring, so how had she ended up with a navel piercing?

Head in her hands, Ronnie considered what the day had in store for her.

Could her brain function properly with this hangover pounding in her head and making her slightly nauseous? She wasn't sure, but she had to at least look like a winner. It didn't matter that she felt terrible—she'd rather die than go on television looking this way.

After a hot shower, ibuprofen and a lot of careful grooming—she slicked her hair back into a ponytail, then braided four sections, which she wove into an elaborate bun at the back of her head—Ronnie showed up at the holding room just in time. She only felt slightly better, but she looked absolutely terrific.

All the chefs and their sous chefs were gathered there before they'd be released to their kitchens to start the competition. As she entered, she found everyone milling around, talking.

"Good morning, Ronnie. How are you feeling?" Ace asked.

As soon as Ronnie saw him, her cheeks started to burn. She'd been so preoccupied that morning, she hadn't taken the time to dwell on her biggest humiliation of the night.

Memories of her tipsy elevator ride, confessing that she was a liar and then throwing herself at Ace all came rushing back.

"Good morning," Ronnie said, hoping that if she pretended not to remember, he might be enough of a gentleman to let the moment pass. "I'm feeling okay," she exaggerated.

He winked at her, leaning down so only she could

hear him. "Got any more goodies tucked away for me to find?"

"Not today," she said through her teeth, as she waved her greetings to the other contestants.

Stewart clapped his hands together. "I hope you came ready to work, people. Because it's going to be tough to beat my authentic French cuisine. I hear Jean Paul Pelletier is one of the judges."

Ann crossed her arms and rolled her eyes. "Oh get off it, Stewart. First of all, I'm more French than you'll ever be. And second, if Jean Paul Pelletier wanted to be fed nothing but French cuisine, he wouldn't have opened a steakhouse in Las Vegas."

Ace laughed out loud. "Besides, this round is about showing off our signature dishes. The judges will be looking to see us do what *we* do best."

Ronnie found herself giggling. "Does that mean you'll be filling the judges up with natural aphrodisiacs, Ace?"

"I don't think it would be a bad idea. They'll be in a really good mood by the time they reach a verdict."

Stewart clapped his hands again, loving to talk trash. "You'll see. I'm classically trained—"

Ann, who was self-taught, shot Stewart a dirty look, freezing the words coming out of his mouth.

"That's enough of all that, now," Etta said, getting up from her seat in the back of the room. "We have to remember that this is still a friendly competition. None of us would be here if we weren't all talented chefs. So let's quiet down now and focus on what's ahead of us."

Etta's voice was as soft and sweet as honey. The room instantly fell silent. Ronnie felt like they'd all just been chastised by their grandmother, so she ducked to the other side of the room to join LQ.

"You don't know how relieved I was to see you walk

through that door," her friend whispered. "You had me in a panic. I called your cell phone three times. I thought you weren't going to show up."

"Are you kidding? This is the big day. I'm ready to win this thing," Ronnie said, trying to sound more confident than she felt.

"All right, boss, that's what I wanted to hear. Should we go over the menu one more time?"

"Go over it in your head. I don't want anyone overhearing our game plan."

Ronnie honestly believed in the integrity of the other chefs in the competition, but something about the intense atmosphere of *this* contest made her wary.

The Las Vegas round of the *All-Star Food Fight* would focus on signature dishes. They would have ninety minutes to create a three-course meal, including a cocktail. The dessert was a no-brainer for Ronnie. Even though she wasn't a pastry chef, she had a knack for desserts. When she worked for the Embassy Plaza hotel, she even made wedding cakes. And in her own restaurant, her chocolate kiss dessert had gotten her a stellar write-up in the *Washington Post*.

Ronnie used a handmade chocolate mold in the shape of lush lips as a frame. Inside, she piped alternating layers of chocolate mousse, crumbled Black Forest cake mixed with a Chambord Liqueur and white-chocolate ganache. Then Ronnie topped the dessert with raspberry puree to make the lips red.

The rest of her menu was carefully designed to complement the dessert. For her cocktail, Ronnie planned to serve a fruity pink drink with coconut rum, pineapple and grenadine. She needed bright, clean flavors to prepare the palate for her rich dessert.

They would start with citrus-glazed scallops for her first

course. Then, for her entrée, she would prepare a lobster tail seasoned with delicate Asian flavors over a crisp cabbage-and-herb salad. She planned to drizzle the plate with just a hint of wasabi oil to add a bit of heat to her dish.

The judges would score them on taste, presentation and originality. On paper, her menu might appear simple, but she'd spent a good deal of time composing the flavors—smoky, citrusy and sweet—so that they unfolded in layers that would keep the judges wanting more.

Ronnie had carefully designed her final plates in her head so that her presentations would have a wow factor. Her scallops and lobster dishes may not score big in originality, but she knew her dessert would bring home all the points she needed in that category.

She and LQ would have to work quickly, in a carefully orchestrated dance to make sure everything was ready on time. But Ronnie believed they could do it. It surprised her how important winning had become over the last few days.

Her confidence would've had a stronger foundation if Ronnie didn't feel sick to her stomach and her belly button didn't sting. What had she been thinking when she'd joined that bachelorette party last night?

Fortunately, there wasn't time to worry over her physical ails as the producer announced that the competition was about to begin. Ronnie and LQ filed out of the holding room and rushed over to their kitchen.

Ronnie knew from past competitions that it was important to stay calm. Cooking under hot studio lights with cameras milling around was a completely different experience from cooking in her own kitchen. Luckily, LQ had done all the previous *Food Fights* with her and knew the drill.

As soon as they got to their kitchen, things started

happening quickly. LQ began pulling together the ingredients for their scallop dish, while Ronnie went right to work on her mold for chocolate lips.

Ronnie had just finished tempering her chocolate when the camera and one of the judges stopped by her kitchen. She raised her head and smiled. As soon as she'd started working, the effects of her hangover were forgotten, and she was in the zone.

"I'm working on my dessert first," she told the camera, "because I need to give the chocolate time to set up in the mold." She went on to describe how she would later fill and present the chocolate kiss when it was ready.

Things were off to a good start, and Ronnie began gaining confidence as she steamed her lobster tails. Then she heard some commotion in the kitchen next to hers.

Over to her left, Stewart beamed as he chattered to the judges about his escargot starter, followed by chateaubriand steak and crème brûlée taken straight off the Compton Arms menu. But the ruckus Ronnie heard originated in Ann Le Marche's kitchen to her right. Ronnie didn't want to get distracted from her own dishes, but Ann was making a fuss that was hard to ignore. Instantly, the camera crew dashed away from Stewart's kitchen to follow Ann.

"Half of my tools are gone," she shouted. Ann was overturning every item in her kitchen, not bothering to stifle her long string of expletives as she stomped around.

Ronnie knew Ann was a student of molecular gastronomy, which relied heavily on science and technology in food preparation. It seemed some of Ann's fancy gadgets had gone missing.

Ronnie just shook her head as she focused on chopping cabbage. Sometimes that happened in competitions. People forgot to pack things or left ingredients off their acquisition list. In times like this, chefs got to prove how well they functioned under pressure.

Just then, LQ leaned over her shoulder. "At the risk of sounding like a copycat…"

Ronnie's back straightened. "What's wrong?"

"Most of our herbs are missing."

"What do you mean? Missing—as in, you forgot to order them?"

"No—as in, I ordered them, but they're not here."

Ronnie resisted the urge to storm around the kitchen, swearing as Ann had just done.

"Okay, this means we're going to have to find another way to flavor the cabbage salad. Take a quick inventory of what we do have, and let's try to put something together."

From there, she and LQ scrambled around the kitchen assessing their options. Ronnie hated to repeat flavors, but they finally agreed that they'd have to use citrus to flavor both the scallops and the cabbage salad that would accompany the lobster. In an effort to switch things up, Ronnie garnished the salad with clementine orange and pink grapefruit supremes.

Even though the colors and flavors were milder than the herb combination she'd planned, Ronnie had to hope she'd done enough to save the dish. Fortunately, her scallop dish was still coming together the way she wanted.

But the clock was ticking down fast, and it was time to check on her chocolate mold. Ronnie knew something was wrong the minute she pulled the refrigerator open.

"LQ, I think it's warm in here." Ronnie pulled out her tray of molds and, sure enough, they were melting all over the pan.

Ronnie heard the cameras zooming in on her station, and

the producer asked her to talk about what was happening. What was happening was that she wanted to cry.

"There seems to be something wrong with my refrigerator. The chocolate lip molds didn't cool, and they're starting to melt."

Ronnie turned to look at LQ, and for the first time in all her years of competing, she wanted to give up and quit. Her chocolate kiss dessert was the star of her meal, and with only fifteen minutes left, there wasn't time to start over from scratch.

Thankfully, LQ remained levelheaded as always. "Okay, we've got to regroup," she said. "What can we do for dessert without the chocolate molds?"

Ronnie inhaled deeply, filling her lungs with air. Suddenly the gears of her mind began to turn. "Find me some cocktail glasses," she told her assistant. "We can still use the filling and make some sort of parfait."

LQ rushed back to her with three martini glasses. Working fast, Ronnie began filling the bottoms of the glasses with chocolate cake. With the refrigerator broken her mousse and ganache were a bit softer than they should be. She just had to hope that the judges would overlook the texture and take the flavors into account.

Topping the desserts with raspberry coulis and chocolate shavings, Ronnie placed them on the serving tray just as the audience counted down to zero.

A loud buzzer sounded, indicating the end of the *Food Fight*. Now they'd each present their dishes to the judges and receive a critique before deliberation and the announcement of the round-one winner.

Ronnie hugged LQ, relieved that, one way or another, it was over. "We made it to the end. Let's just hope we've done enough to make it past this round."

* * *

Ace clapped his assistant, Marcel, on the back. "It was touch-and-go there for a few minutes, buddy, but I think we did our thing."

Marcel slapped his hand, sliding his fingers back into a snap. "We've got this, Ace. I just know we've got this."

Ace was glad to be the first to present his dishes to the judges. Marcel went back to the holding room to watch everything on a big-screen TV with the other chefs, while Ace went to stand on his mark.

The director gave him his cue to start.

"Well, I'm known as the Sexy Chef, so I had to prepare some sexy dishes for you today. To start, I have oysters three ways. The first one is in a half shell flavored with yuzu juice, the second is fried crispy in brown butter and chives and the third is a sweet ceviche."

Ace was really pleased with the way his three courses had turned out, but it didn't happen without a bit of Las Vegas's Lady Luck on his side. A few ingredients were missing and the oven in his kitchen cooked unevenly, but improvisation saved the day.

He hadn't planned on serving a fried oyster, but when he couldn't count on his oven to heat properly, he switched his game plan. The results turned out even better than he'd hoped.

"For the entrée, I've given you a beautiful seared filet of beef with a trio of sauces to dip it in. My specialty is meals for two, but since there are three of you, I've made three the theme for the day."

Ace knew the judges didn't give any points for charm, but he was hoping it wouldn't hurt. Especially since he was afraid his dessert plate was looking a bit empty. It was supposed to be filled with a triple-layer chocolate cake, but again the oven had forced him to change things up.

"And to finish this meal off, I've given you a trio of chocolate truffles. For a bit of variation on the signature cocktail, I decided to offer you a hot coffee shot with brandy and Kahlúa."

Ace kept a smile on his face as the judges sampled his offerings. "The truffles were delicious," said Jean Paul Pelletier. "My only complaint is that I wish there had been more. Perhaps you could have added some coulis or sauce so the plate didn't look so sparse."

The next judge, renowned pastry chef Kari Voegler, told him that his team did the best at regrouping from some major setbacks, and the final judge, Hawaiian restaurateur Sam Lomi, complimented Ace's flavors and his creativity.

Overall, Ace went back into the holding room feeling pretty good. But his heart went out to Ronnie when it was her turn to stand before the judges.

She was his competition, and Ace should have been glad that they were a bit tougher on Ronnie, but he couldn't help but hope she would make it past the first round.

He watched the screen as the cameraman zoomed in on Ronnie's face as Judge Lomi spoke. "I really enjoyed the flavors of your dish. But I can't help thinking it lacked a bit of creativity to have the same flavors in both your appetizer and your entrée."

Ronnie simply nodded. "Yes, of course. I planned to flavor the entrée with an herb salad, but some of our herbs were missing."

"And I'm not sure what this dessert is supposed to be," Judge Voegler said, dissecting the contents of the martini glass with her spoon. "Everything is mushy and running together."

"But you have to admit it does taste good," Judge Pelletier chimed in.

Minutes later, Ronnie walked back into the holding room looking a bit like a deflated balloon. Ace wanted to go over and comfort her, but he had a strong suspicion that any words from him wouldn't be welcome.

"This is BS," Ann Le Marche shouted as she entered the room after her critique. "Did anyone else have supplies missing or appliances that didn't work?"

Everyone in the room raised their hands, which Ann followed with another string of expletives.

"What kind of rinky-dink operation are they running here? This is my fifth *Food Fight* for GTV, and I've never had so many things go wrong."

Stewart shrugged. "Maybe they did it on purpose. You know, to see how we handle the pressure. We all showed up with prepared menus. Maybe they threw a monkey into the works to make the competition more exciting."

"I think the expression is monkey *wrench,* dear," Etta offered.

"Whatever. The point is, either you pulled it off or you didn't. Since we all had some sort of trouble, it's probably safe to assume it was part of the competition."

Ann glared at Stewart from across the room, then threw her hands up. From where he sat, Ace could still hear her cursing the air blue around her.

After all the contestants received their critiques, they would normally line up for the presentation of the award check. But since this competition would continue for two more rounds, each chef was sent back to their kitchens to hear their scores. For the chef with the lowest score, their kitchen would go dark, and they'd be eliminated from the competition.

As Ace stood next to Marcel in his kitchen, he felt pretty good about his chances. It surprised him how concerned he was that Ronnie might not continue to the next round.

"With the highest score in the competition, earning a total of forty-four out of fifty, our round-one leader is Etta Foster." The in-studio audience clapped and cheered.

"Second, with a score of thirty-two out of fifty, is Ace Brown."

Ace felt Marcel patting him on the back, saying, "Hawaii, here we come!"

Ace nodded absently. They were in a pretty good position heading into the next round, but he couldn't keep himself from turning toward Ronnie's kitchen on the other side of Stewart.

The host was just awarding Stewart Compton third place. Suddenly the music in the studio got louder as the spotlights focused on Ronnie and Ann's kitchens.

"One of these remaining contestants will be moving on to the second round in Hawaii, and the other will be going home. The contestant coming in fourth, with a total score of twenty-six out of fifty is Veronica Howard. That means Ann Le Marche has been eliminated from the competition with a total score of twenty-two out of fifty."

Ace watched Ronnie hug LQ and felt more relieved than he should have. But the fact was, he and Ronnie had a lot of unfinished business.

She'd been very tipsy when she'd kissed him last night, but that didn't mean she wasn't expressing all the feelings she kept on lockdown when she was sober. Now that she'd tipped her hand, Ace planned to press that advantage.

Chapter 7

For several minutes after the rankings were announced, Ronnie's heart continued to pound in her chest. She'd been convinced that she and LQ were going home. The judges' comments about her dishes had been disappointing at best. Sure, her dessert was mushy and the flavors in her entrée weren't as unique as they should have been, but she stood behind the fact that everything tasted really good.

"Cheer up," LQ said. "We'll do better next time. At least we made it through to the next round."

"Barely."

"I know you're disappointed in our final score, but this is the *All-Star Food Fight.* It's supposed to be more of a challenge."

"A challenge is one thing. Outright sabotage is another. Do you think the network screwed up our kitchens on purpose?"

LQ shrugged. "Normally, I'd say no. But, since everyone had complaints, it's starting to look that way."

Ronnie shook her head, uncertain what to believe. "Do we have any cocktails left? I could use one."

"Honey, I don't know what you did last night, but judging from the way you were first moving when you got here this morning, you should probably lay off the cocktails."

"I was just kidding," Ronnie said, then suddenly looked up as Ace entered the kitchen.

"Congratulations, ladies."

Ronnie sighed. "Did you come over here to gloat?"

Ace laughed. "It's not time for that yet. I just wanted to invite you two to join Marcel and me for dinner tonight to celebrate."

Ronnie frowned. "You two have reason to celebrate. We don't."

"Oh come on, you made it to Hawaii. That's worth celebrating."

LQ stepped forward. "I can't make it anyway. I have tickets to see the magician at the Monte Carlo tonight. It's a VIP package that includes dinner and a backstage meet-and-greet."

"Then I guess it's just you and me, Ronnie," Ace said.

"What about Marcel?"

"I'd hate to make him feel like a third wheel. Besides, I have tickets to a show, too, and Marcel definitely won't go with me."

Ronnie turned away to gather her things. "No, I think I'd better stay in tonight. I did enough celebrating last night to last me awhile."

"Come on, didn't you say there were three things you wanted to do in Vegas before you left? Tonight is your chance."

"I don't know," she said, packing up her knives. "I'm really not in the mood."

"All the more reason to go. Don't sit around in your

room rehashing the competition. It's over. There's time to focus on what's up ahead tomorrow. Tonight, enjoy Las Vegas."

Ronnie knew everything Ace was saying was true. But, going out on the town last night had made her lose focus for today's competition. Maybe the best thing to do was keep a low profile and stay on track.

"I've cleaned up everything, Ronnie. I'll see you tomorrow," LQ said, interrupting her thoughts. "And, for what it's worth, you *should* go out tonight. Have a nice dinner and put today behind you."

"There it is," Ace said. "LQ agrees with me. You're outnumbered, two against one."

Ronnie threw her hands up in surrender. "Fine. I'll have dinner with you tonight."

Chapter 8

When Ace got back to his hotel room, he felt like he was on top of the world. Not only had he come in second in the *All-Star Food Fight,* he'd gotten Ronnie to agree to go out with him. Now he had just one more detail to take care of, he thought, picking up the phone.

"Fontaine here," Garett answered.

"I need a huge favor."

"Ah, a favor. I love it when you owe me."

"Great, because I need you to get me two really good seats to a show for tonight."

Garett paused for a moment. "Short notice, great seats… This is going to cost you."

"I'm willing to pay. I just need to know if you can do it."

"Depends on the show. What do you want to see?"

Ace shrugged, looking around his room as he tried to remember what was popular. "I don't know. What's hot?"

"Hot? How about *Le Nu?*"

"What's that?"

Garett chuckled. "It's like a cross between a French revue and Cirque du Soleil."

"That sounds perfect. Get me the best seats you can."

"I'll do my best, but first, can I ask just why you want me to bust my hump getting these tickets?"

Ace smiled. "I have a date tonight."

"Let me guess. It's with one Ms. Veronica Howard?"

"That's right."

"You should let me make the most of this occasion. You get to impress Ronnie with great seats to a hot show, and I can get a little free publicity to promote your new cookbook. It's win-win."

Ace shook his head. "What are you talking about?"

"I'll tip off a couple of photographers and tomorrow on TMZ everyone will be talking about the celebrity chef who's having a bit of a showmance on the set of GTV's *All-Star Food Fight.*"

"There you go again. What does 'showmance' even mean?"

"Just what it sounds like. A romance on the set of a reality show."

Ace rolled his eyes. "I hardly think the press would take an interest in anything going on between a couple of chefs from Gourmet TV. It's a bad idea on so many levels."

"Why don't you let me be the judge of that?"

Ace's thoughts were already moving on to dinner reservations. "What I want you to do is get me those tickets. That's all I need right now."

He hung up with Garett and, just as he'd hoped, twenty minutes later he received a text message confirming that the tickets would be waiting for him at the box office.

Now he just had to confirm the evening's plans with Ronnie, he thought, dialing her room number.

"Why don't we meet in the lobby at six so we can have dinner," Ace suggested when Ronnie picked up the phone.

"Actually, I think it might be best if I stay in tonight."

"Stay in? But I have front-row seats to one of the hottest shows in town."

Ronnie sighed. "Well, the problem is that I only brought one party dress, and I wore it last night. I'm not exaggerating when I say I have nothing to wear. Unless you want to set a new fashion trend of chefs' jackets as evening wear."

"You don't have anything to wear? Is that the only problem?"

Ronnie hesitated. "Well, yeah…"

"Fine, that's easily remedied. Let's go shopping at Caesars."

"*Let's?* You actually want to go with me? I'm sure I could pick something out myself. I just don't know if it's worth the effort."

"Why not?"

"Because I hate shopping."

Ace laughed. "You're the first woman I've ever heard say that."

"Well, it's true. I think I would rather wear my chef's jacket than skulk around a mall trying to find something to wear," she said grimly.

"Then consider me your personal shopper. I promise to make it fun."

"Thanks for the offer," she said, and Ace could hear that he was losing her. "But, I really should stay in tonight."

"Come on. I'll make the experience as painless as

possible," he said, refusing to take no for an answer. "Meet me in the lobby in fifteen minutes."

Before Ronnie could protest again, Ace hung up the phone.

As soon as she put down the phone, Ronnie began pacing her hotel room. Shopping? With Ace? She felt anxiety rising in her chest.

Even though she no longer wore plus-size clothes, all the memories of fluorescent lights and unflattering mirror images came rushing back to her. She wouldn't even have had her one party dress if Cara hadn't insisted that she pick out a goal outfit that she wanted to fit into when she lost weight.

Despite her worries over going shopping, there was one strong feeling overpowering that fear. And it was the desire to spend time with Ace.

She was completely embarrassed by her behavior the night before, but Ace didn't seem to be the least bit put off by it. In fact, now that she'd made a fool of herself gushing over him, he seemed even more determined to spend time with her.

It would have been nice if Ace could have shown this kind of interest in her when she was overweight, but she wasn't going to dwell on that now. She couldn't blame him for preferring the skinnier Ronnie over the heavier version. After all, she had no trouble appreciating his buff physique then or now.

Realizing that she would be running late if she continued to wallow in her emotions, she picked up her purse and headed to the lobby.

Ace had been right about one thing. Sitting in her room fretting over all the things that had gone wrong that day wouldn't do her any good. As she rode the elevator down to the lobby, she vowed to live in the moment and enjoy her night out. The shopping? That still remained to be seen.

Ace and Ronnie walked over to the mall in Caesars Palace hotel, and he directed her to an upscale women's clothing store.

As soon as they crossed the threshold, Ronnie felt her heartbeat pick up speed. She took in all the skinny metallic mannequins and felt certain that nothing in the store would look good on her. How was she going to get out of this? But before she could make a break for the door, Ace had already motioned for a sales clerk to come over.

"May I help you?"

"Yes, this beautiful lady needs a dress for an evening on the town. Can you offer her some suggestions?"

Immediately Ronnie felt like her cheeks were on fire. She expected the saleswoman to turn a disapproving look in her direction and laugh her out of the store. To make matters worse, the woman had the nerve to ask the dreaded question.

"What size do you wear?"

Ronnie swallowed hard. "Uh…I…um—" Her old dress size formed on her lips and she stumbled over the number as she realized she didn't wear double digits anymore.

"You look like a four. Let me pull some dresses for you."

"No, I don't think…four?"

"If the fours are too big, I'll bring you a smaller size."

Ronnie was shaking her head as the saleswoman returned with three dresses and led her over to a dressing room. Taking the dresses Ronnie entered the room feeling like a caged animal. In a few minutes she'd have to come back out and admit that none of the dresses fit her. Worse yet, she'd have to admit this truth in front of Ace.

At a loss for any other option, Ronnie took the first dress off the rack in the fitting room. It was a red sheath that made her cringe in anticipation. But because it didn't have any belts and wasn't cinched at the waist, she tried to pull it over her head.

To her shock the dress slid over her figure with room to spare. Before Ronnie could turn to check the mirror, Ace's voice came through the door.

"Come out and let me see it."

Ronnie's eyes went wide and she spun to look in the mirror. She blinked, not recognizing the thin but curvy woman looking back at her.

A woman who wore a size four.

The dress hung from a beaded halter at the neck to skim over her hips, ending just above her knees. Stepping forward, Ronnie opened the dressing-room door just enough for Ace to catch a glimpse of the dress.

"I can't see you. Step all the way out."

Tiptoeing forward, Ronnie watched his eyes light up as he took her in. He was already nodding as he motioned for her to spin around. Ronnie started to protest, but he looked so pleased by the sight of her, she couldn't resist.

"Very sexy."

Ronnie's cheeks were on fire once again, but this time for a different reason. She'd never had a man tell her she was sexy before.

Feeling almost giddy, Ronnie disappeared into the dressing room and put on the next dress. This one was a royal-blue strapless that hid nothing from breast to hip. The fabric was beautifully draped with ruching at the waist, but Ronnie feared it was too revealing.

As soon as she stepped out of the dressing room, Ace and the sales girl began oohing and ahhing.

"Ronnie, you look incredible in that dress."

"That's the perfect color for you," the sales girl said, "and it really compliments your figure."

Ronnie immediately discounted the clerk's opinion because Ronnie knew the girl wanted to make a sale. But Ace's appreciation was written all over his face. He looked like he wanted to scoop Ronnie up and rush her back to his room.

Suddenly this shopping experience had taken a turn for the better. Ronnie went back into the dressing room and put on dress number three. It was a black lacy number with spaghetti straps and a frilled hemline.

"This dress looks great," Ace said when she came out of the dressing room, "but the blue one's my favorite. It, um, showed off your best assets."

Ronnie eyed him up and down. "My best assets? And what would those be?" she teased, enjoying watching him squirm.

For a second she saw him racking his brain for a politically correct answer until he saw the evil glint in her eye. They both laughed.

She put her hand on her hip. "I don't know. The blue dress may be dangerous to my virtue. Maybe I ought to shop around for something more conservative?"

Ace waved off that suggestion. "Nah, you hate shopping. The blue dress is perfect. If you don't buy it for yourself, I'm buying it for you."

Ronnie felt her heart float with feminine pride. "You like it that much, huh?"

He winked at her and she suddenly felt as though she was standing before him naked. "Okay, fine, I'll buy the blue dress."

"Maybe you should get the red and black, too. After all, I'm going to want to take you out in Hawaii and Paris."

Ronnie sighed. Not only was he making it clear that he planned to spend a lot of time with her in the future, he was also expressing confidence that she'd make it to the final round of *Food Fight*.

She was riding so high from all the positive feedback, Ronnie decided she would buy the other dresses, as well. After all, it couldn't hurt to be prepared.

Ace walked her back to the hotel and they parted ways to get ready for the evening. She'd been so consumed by the shopping trip that she hadn't even asked him what show they'd be going to see.

Later, as Ronnie slipped into her blue dress, she thought about her most recent dating history. It had been a long time since she'd been on a date. But now that she'd allowed herself the indulgence, she was going to make sure she enjoyed it.

Seeing Andre at the press junket yesterday had reminded her of what a fool she'd been. But what she saw in the mirror today reminded her that she wasn't that person anymore. Why couldn't she have a good time with an old friend? Sure, he was a notorious player, but she wasn't ready for anything long term anyway.

Ronnie decided she was going to revel in this relationship for as long as she lasted in the competition. She'd enjoyed watching Ace's eyes pop out of his head when he'd seen her in that blue dress.

Leaning forward, she applied a hint of sparkle to her eyelids. Tonight she wasn't above tempting him a little further. And if things progressed between them, she wasn't going to hold herself back.

Ace waited in the lobby for Ronnie, anxious to get the night started. When she stepped off the elevator, he suddenly sucked his lungs full of air, as if he'd just been punched in the gut. Even though he'd seen her try on the dress in the store, nothing had prepared him for the full effect with hair and makeup. She'd pulled just enough hair back from her face to show off her bright, shimmering eyes and a pair of glittering earrings. The rest of her hair curled down her back in soft waves, just above her shoulders.

Without any other jewelry to disrupt his view, his eyes traveled down her bare neck to her ample cleavage and got lost there. A second later, Ronnie snapped her fingers in front of his face.

"Hey, Ace, my eyes are up here."

"Yes, but I've seen *those* before." Then his skin heated as he realized he wasn't acting like the gentleman he'd set out to be. "I'm sorry," he chuckled. "I wasn't supposed to say that out loud."

Fortunately, when he raised his eyes to hers, he saw that she didn't look angry. In fact, her eyes held a flirtatious glimmer as she reached up and touched his cheek.

"Getting fresh on the first date?" she asked.

He leaned down and kissed her on the cheek, inhaling her soft floral scent. "You can't blame a guy for trying. I mean, look at you. It's not my fault that I temporarily lost control of my common sense."

Ronnie laughed. "Saved by the charm once again."

Ace took Ronnie to the brand-new luxury hotel on the Strip where the show *Le Nu* was playing. He'd had the concierge make reservations at the five-star restaurant there.

As the host led them to their table, Ronnie turned to look at Ace, her eyes flashing with anticipation. "I've heard so much about the chef of this restaurant. I've been dying to try his seafood risotto. You must be really connected to get last-minute reservations."

Instantly, Ace knew he had a way to redeem himself for his lecherous behavior earlier. When Ronnie went to the ladies' room, he signaled the waiter to send a message to the chef.

When she returned, they shared a crab cake appetizer and found themselves laughing about Ann Le Marche's cursing fit during the competition.

When it was time for their entrées to be served, Ace could barely hide his smile as he saw Chef Telloni headed in their direction.

Ronnie's back straightened and her eyes opened wide as the chef stopped at their table. "I hear you would like to try my seafood risotto," he said, after introducing himself to her.

"Yes, I would." She looked across to Ace. "How did you know?"

Chef Telloni clapped Ace on the back. "Ace and I are old friends. And he tells me you're a remarkable chef yourself."

"Does he, now? I can never get him to admit it to me, but I'm glad to hear that he knows it."

"Come this way, and I will give you the VIP tour."

The chef led Ronnie back into the kitchen, put her in an apron and showed them how he made his seafood risotto. Of course, with some of the ingredients already prepped, his real secrets remained intact. But Ace knew Ronnie was thrilled with the experience.

When they returned to their table, the waiter served them the very dishes they had just watched Chef Telloni prepare, and Ronnie was on cloud nine.

"Do you have room for dessert?"

Ronnie looked wistfully at the menu. "I'm going to have to get up early and work out twice as hard if I do."

"Come on, a little chocolate never hurt anyone."

She shook her head. "Speak for yourself. A little choc-olate here and a little chocolate there, and picture me eighty pounds heavier."

Ace knew she was probably sensitive about her weight, so he wasn't sure of the best way to respond. Fortunately, she continued on her own.

"I'm sure you understand. You didn't get that buff in your sleep, did you? If you tell me your muscles just sprout out of nowhere because of your naturally fast metabolism, I'm going to get up and leave."

"No, you're right. I try to do some form of exercise every day. I slacked a little while I was traveling, and I had to spend more than a couple of weeks in the gym to get back into shape."

She smiled. "After all, the Sexy Chef has a lot to live up to."

"How about I make you a deal? We'll split a dessert, and I'll work out with you in the morning."

"You'll work out with me, huh? Just what kind of exercise did you have in mind?"

Ace grinned. She was flirting with him again. "Any kind you think you can handle."

Then the waiter came and interrupted them before things got out of hand. Ace ordered a fruit-and-sorbet platter for them to share.

Before the waiter could walk away, she said to Ace, "Wait a minute. I thought you wanted a little chocolate."

He gave her a puzzled look. "I thought you wanted to be health conscious."

"But this restaurant is famous for its Grand Marnier cake and chocolate gelato."

He gestured to the waiter and changed their order.

Ronnie shrugged. "If I'm going to have to double my workout, I may as well make sure it's worth it."

Minutes later the waiter returned with their dessert and the two of them wasted no time tucking into it.

"Uh, Ace, you have whipped cream on your cheek."

He winked at her. "Want to lick it off for me?"

Her nose instantly wrinkled. "I'm sorry, but you may as well know, despite the fact that I'm a chef, I don't go for all that licking food off body parts. It grosses me out."

Ace wiped his cheek with his napkin. "Are you kidding me? You don't like a little chocolate and whipped cream in the bedroom?"

She wrinkled her face again, shaking her head vigorously.

"You don't know what you're missing," he said, licking his fork clean.

"I'm sorry but food tastes best when eaten off plates. Once you mix in salty skin, the whole recipe is thrown off."

"Maybe you just haven't tried the right combination of person and food."

Ace hadn't meant to let his thoughts go there, but suddenly in his mind's eye he saw Ronnie spread out and covered with whipped cream, chocolate and strawberries, and his entire body went hot. He had to focus on his breathing so he wouldn't start panting and give his thoughts away.

"I have too much respect for food to treat it that way."

His eyes narrowed with skepticism. "You're making it sound like you've never even tried it."

"I don't have to. When I was seventeen, my best friend Cara and I snuck into this racy movie that was famous for its sexy love scenes. Well, in one of them, the guy puts the girl on the floor in front of the refrigerator and just starts pulling stuff out and smearing it all over her."

Ronnie absently licked her fork as she spoke passionately. "Trust me when I tell you, it was *not* sexy."

Tell that to my pants, Ace thought, chewing on the inside of his mouth to rein in his libido.

Not only were her words sexy to him, she wasn't even aware of the way she'd taken a bite of cake and then licked every speck of chocolate off her fork with the tip of her tongue. Even the most proper gentlemen would have had trouble resisting that image.

"And," Ronnie continued, "if I'm reading your face correctly, let me just warn you now, do not take my words as a personal challenge. You'll never convince me otherwise. The whole idea makes me sick."

Caught in the act, Ace made a show of looking at his watch. "The show will be starting soon. We'd better finish up."

Grateful to have a safe topic to focus on, his amorous thoughts eventually began to abate. After starting off this date with such a sexually charged conversation, it would be a great relief to clear his mind for a couple of hours during the show.

Ronnie walked with Ace through the hotel to the theater where the show would take place. As they approached the doors, she saw a series of posters with performers covered in elaborate body paint inside flaming rings, suspended in swings and walking tightropes.

"Le Nu?" she asked. "I don't think I've heard anything about this show. What's it about?"

"Honestly, I'm not sure. But Garett said that it's the hottest ticket in town."

She shrugged. "I guess I haven't heard anything about it because it's a new production."

An usher escorted them to their seats three rows from

the stage. "These *are* great seats. I guess it's all about who you know."

"In that case, I know Garett, and he knows everyone else."

Ronnie laughed and relaxed back into her seat. It amazed her how easy this date was. Normally, even when she tried her best to relax, she found relationships to be a lot of work. Granted, they were only a few hours into the date, but Ace was courteous, complimentary and seemed genuinely attracted to her. There was no chance that at the end of this date he would tell her he just wanted to be friends.

On the contrary, the sexual tension between them seemed to be mounting quickly. She couldn't believe that they'd gotten comfortable enough to actually talk about sex. Thank goodness they had this show to keep their minds on neutral ground for an hour or two.

After several minutes, the theater went dark and a ringmaster stepped through the curtain to begin the show. As he began introducing performers, Ronnie started to realize that, despite the fancy body paint, all the performers were naked.

The body art was done tastefully, and the circus acts required skill and training, but the nudity created a sensuality that was normally absent from similar performances she'd seen in the past.

Ace leaned toward her and whispered in her ear, "I'm sorry. I didn't know."

Ronnie felt her skin flushing profusely. "It's okay."

"I just heard the guy next to me tell his wife that *le nu* means *the naked* in French. I'm going to kill Garett when I see him."

"Really, it's okay. The show isn't raunchy or tasteless. Let's just enjoy it."

But as the show went on, Ronnie found it increasingly

difficult to focus on the performance. Instead she was excruciatingly aware of Ace's every move beside her. Anytime his hand or arm brushed hers she felt her skin burn.

On the stage, a male and a female with perfectly sculpted bodies entwined and contorted as they swept around in a sultry dance.

Ronnie felt like her entire body was on alert. Finally, it was clear that Ace had given up pretending he wasn't affected by the titillating sights before them. He slipped his arm around her and began caressing her shoulder.

She leaned into him as much as she could despite the armrest separating them. Her nipples had constricted so tightly they were almost painful.

As she concentrated on not moaning in pleasure at his caress, his fingers glided up from her bare shoulder to slip beneath her hair. He rubbed her neck in soft little circles that caused her eyelids to close involuntarily.

It seemed like an eternity passed before the show was over. Ronnie watched, half-distracted by Ace's presence as a sensual array of music and beautiful bodies assaulted her senses.

Neither of them said a word as they left the theater. Ace hailed a cab back to their hotel, and during the short ride, they sat close to each other, still barely speaking.

Even though it had been hours since she'd had any wine, Ronnie felt drunk. Her entire body was heavy, from her eyelids to her legs. They felt as though they'd been weighed down with lead.

They walked through the lobby and rode the elevator together. Ronnie punched in her floor, and Ace made no move to choose his own.

Her heart began to pound in her chest with anticipation. Part of her felt like she should slow things down, or weigh the pros and cons of the moment, but that part of her was receding tonight.

Ronnie pulled out her key, and Ace followed her into the room. Before she could get too far, he lifted her against his body and crushed his mouth over hers in a long, deep kiss.

Chapter 9

When the kiss broke, Ace smiled and said, "I've been wanting to do that all day."

Ronnie leaned into him. "Then next time, don't wait so long," she said, running her tongue across her upper lip. Their kiss had ended her fast and now she wanted more.

She lifted her face to his, but his head was already lowering again. This time, his lips pressed hers at a much less urgent pace. Inviting his slow exploration, she let her lips part naturally so his tongue could slip between them.

Hunger fully awakened, Ronnie *was* feeling a sense of urgency. These kisses were just an aperitif, and she wanted to skip to the main course. Three years of celibacy were now working against her as her supersensitive skin tingled for his touch.

Ace's mouth continued its slow, gentle brushes against hers. Pressing back with more force, Ronnie had to restrain herself from devouring him like a woman famished.

Reaching up to hook her arms around his neck, she let her fingers trace upward to his cleanly shaven head. The movement pulled her body tighter against his. The material of her gown scraped her aching nipples as her generous breasts threatened to pull free from the dress.

But suddenly her clothes no longer mattered. Ace was fingering the zipper under her right arm. With a quick downward flick, the dress fell to her feet, leaving Ronnie in nothing but a pair of panties and heels.

She hadn't been stripped bare before a man since she'd lost weight. Resisting the urge to cover herself, instead she splayed her arms as though she were an all-you-can-eat buffet. Whether Ace liked what he saw or not, it was too late for her to make any changes. And she had too much pride to cower under his heated gaze.

Lifting her chin to bolster confidence, she raised her eyes to take in his reaction. To Ronnie's relief, if she were an all-you-can-eat buffet, Ace was a man with a hearty appetite.

His eyes drank her in and his lips parted as though his mouth watered for the taste of her. A guttural sound escaped his throat. "My God, you're sexy," he growled.

Ronnie, trembled slightly, wobbling on her heels. Could it be that this beefy hunk of man really wanted her?

As his hooded gaze burned over her, the bulge in his slacks grew, confirming the truth of his words.

Ronnie had never felt so beautiful or powerful.

He reached out and touched the jewelry in her belly button. "This is a surprise."

"To me, too. A little souvenir from the bachelorette party," she whispered.

"I like it," he whispered back.

Feeling bold, she stripped off her underwear. The scrap

of fabric had barely hit the floor before Ace lunged forward and swung her up into his arms.

He carried her to the bedroom and placed her gently on the bed. Ace tore away his coat and shirt, but he didn't pause for her to take in each ripple of muscle or the dark-roasted-coffee color of his skin. His hands worked quickly to satisfy the raw need that was etched out on his features. Off came his pants and underwear before Ace went in search of protection.

Once he found it, he crawled onto the bed, raising himself up on his knees before her. Finally, Ronnie could take in the feast.

The only light was the twinkling city shimmer streaming in through the windows. But it was enough for her to see that Ace had a lot to be proud of. He was broad and solid, from his linebacker torso to his powerful thighs.

Then his hard, heavy form came down on top of her, as Ace slowly entered her, gently yielding to allow her to fully accommodate his size.

Ronnie stretched her fingers and came into contact with the soft, springy hair on the hard planes of his chest. She let her nails flick his small, peaked nipples before striking out to explore his slatted abs.

Ace took her mouth in hungry bites, first a corner, then a lip. Then their tongues found each other. Meanwhile, his hands were sampling the buffet, cupping her breasts, stroking her waist, caressing her hips.

Ronnie's thoughts became hazy as sensations began to layer like the flavors of a rich sauce. She tasted his salty-sweet skin from his neck to his toes. Her eyes feasted on his physical perfection.

As Ace's caresses became more intimate, she remembered how long it had been since she'd been with a man like this.

Then he whispered, "I want you so badly," while sipping at her neck. Folded against his larger, muscular body, Ronnie felt petite and dainty. And she knew she'd never been with a man quite like this. He was focused on her pleasure, each touch attentive and loving. He made her feel like the only woman in his world.

Her hands roamed his broad back, while his large hands molded the cheeks of her round derriere, pulling her close until there was no more space between them. Their bodies paired like a filet and fine wine, each bringing out the best in the other.

Ronnie heard her breath coming heavily as her anticipation mounted. An ache began to grow in her core, and she craved more of Ace, unable to get enough of him.

"Ace, please," she pleaded against his mouth.

He continued to feed her lust with quick, hard strokes. She bit her lip, as he turned up the heat. Then, just as Ronnie thought she could take no more, she reached her boiling point. The pressure inside her released like steam in a kettle, and Ace followed seconds after.

After a moment, their bodies began to cool, and Ace withdrew, kissing her gently on the cheek.

With a sigh, Ronnie fell back against the pillows, her appetite fully satisfied.

Ace watched Ronnie come awake. Before her eyes opened, her body uncurled and she stretched one arm above her head. Then her lashes fluttered, and he found himself staring into her dark brown eyes.

There was a moment of disorientation, then a slow smile curved her lips as she focused on his face.

"Good morning," he said jovially, leaning forward to press his lips against hers.

Ronnie accepted the kiss then glanced away shyly. "Good morning. I feel like I slept like the dead. What time is it?"

"Almost noon," he answered, laughing, watching her expression change from shy to startled.

She sat up straight in bed. "Noon? I'm a morning person. I never sleep this late."

Ace was neither a morning nor a night person. He'd actually been a bit of an insomniac lately, waking early and going to bed late. But with Ronnie in his arms, he couldn't remember the last time he'd slept so soundly.

"I guess I really wore you out," he teased.

She grinned at him. "I think I gave as good as I got."

He nodded. Ace was in a fantastic mood and Ronnie was one hundred percent the reason. And he wanted to let her know that.

"Seriously, Ronnie. Last night was incredible. I've wanted to be with you for so long."

She snorted. "So long? A whole three days?"

"No, not just three days. I've wanted to be with you since culinary school."

Ronnie scoffed. "Come on, Ace. You don't have to do this. I don't need you to throw me a line or pretend this means more than it does. You gave me just what I needed. It was great. We can leave it at that."

Ace frowned, stunned at her reaction. "Wait a minute. I don't think you're hearing me."

"I hear you. And I'm letting you off the hook. I'm done looking at relationships through rose-colored glasses. We had fun. Now the only thing I need to know is how this is going to affect the next leg of the competition. You're not going to go all soft just because we slept together, are you?"

Ace's spine straightened. He wanted to argue. He'd had

feelings for Ronnie from the very beginning, but she didn't want to believe it. He knew she had a rocky history with men. Trying to convince her that he really cared about her was probably futile at this point.

The only way to let Ronnie know how he felt would be to show her. And he was more than willing to put forth the effort.

"Do me a favor," he said, "and don't mention *soft* and *sleeping together* in the same breath. And you don't have to worry about the competition. I always bring my A game. I expect you to do the same."

"Don't worry, I will. And don't get complacent just because I'm in fourth place right now. You haven't seen the best of me yet."

Ace laughed, thinking back to all of the trash-talking they used to do in school. "I'm sure that's true. The problem is, even your best isn't as good as my worst."

Her eyes went wide. "Oh, is that so? It's been many years since we've cooked in the same kitchen. You have no idea what new tricks I've learned."

He lay back on the pillows folding his arms behind his head, feeling confident. "That's true. I've seen how you cook in the bedroom, and I have no complaints there. But you have to remember, I've sharpened my knives in kitchens around the world. You haven't seen all *my* best moves either, in the kitchen or the bedroom."

She narrowed her eyes at him. "Oh, you'll be lucky if you get a repeat performance in the bedroom."

Ace sat up, clutching the sheets to his chest in mock outrage. "You're not telling me this was just a one-night stand, are you? I think you should know I'm not that kind of guy!"

Ronnie picked up her pillow and bonked him on the head. "Stop being so silly," she said, glancing at the clock.

"Oh, no, the day is getting away from me. I have to hit the gym and then get back here to pack for the flight to Hawaii this evening. When are you leaving?"

"First thing tomorrow morning."

She started to climb out of bed, and Ace, realizing he wasn't ready to leave her presence, took her wrist and pulled her close. "Are you sure I can't persuade you to stay here in bed with me?"

"I don't know."

He leaned down, dropping kisses on her neck.

"It is a tempting offer."

He started massaging her shoulders.

She squirmed in his embrace. "You have to stop that. I can hardly think straight."

"That's the idea."

"You don't understand. Cara's going to call and ask me if I made it to the gym while I was here, and if I can't honestly tell her that I did, she won't leave me alone."

"Some might consider what we did last night a workout," he said, placing a kiss on her throat.

She hit him in the stomach with her pillow.

"Never mind. How about you sleep in with me and just tell her you worked out."

"There's a good reason I did so poorly at the poker tables the other night. Apparently, I have a tell and Cara's very familiar with it."

"A tell, huh?" Ronnie could be hard to read. So if she had a reliable habit that tipped her hand, Ace needed to identify it. "What is it?"

"Oh, no, I'm not telling you. You're just going to have to figure that one out on your own."

"Fine. If you won't join me, I'll join you in the gym just like I promised. Afterward maybe we can grab a late lunch."

"I wouldn't mind having a workout buddy, but I can't do lunch. I have to meet up with LQ later. I'll probably just order room service to eat while I pack."

"All right, then why don't we have dinner together tomorrow night in Kauai?"

Ronnie hesitated.

He wagged his finger at her. "If you don't go out with me again, I'm going to feel used."

"Fine, you big baby. Dinner, but don't count on dessert. We'll have to see about that."

Chapter 10

Ronnie dressed in her sweats and took the elevator to the gym to meet Ace. As soon as she set foot inside the pristine high-tech gym, she regretted agreeing to let Ace join her.

While the gym itself was amazing, offering a huge selection of fancy machines, free bottled water and indoor rock-climbing, the atmosphere was already making her want to run back to her room.

All the women were scantily clad hard-bodies that made her wish she'd done more than throw on a baggy T-shirt and frumpy cutoff sweatpants. And her ponytail wasn't cutting it either. If you wanted to work out in this gym, you needed full hair and makeup to match your designer workout clothes.

Ronnie might have bailed out completely if Ace hadn't chosen that very moment to come up behind her. "There you are. Ready to break a sweat?"

She turned to see Ace dressed in a sleeveless gray T-shirt

and long white basketball shorts. The outfit was nothing special, but he definitely made it look good. Maybe they should have slept in after all.

"Yeah, but I don't know how long I'm going to stay. Maybe I'll just run on the treadmill for a few minutes."

"Sounds good. Let's do it."

Ronnie programmed her machine, watching as he matched her settings. "Um, don't let me hold you back. I concentrate on fat burning rather than cardio." She winced. Did she really just say *fat burning* out loud? That was just great. Remind him that she had a lot of fat to burn. Not sexy at all.

"No problem. This is a great warm-up and we'll still be able to talk to each other."

Wishing the treadmill would allow her to run away rather than stay in one spot, Ronnie started a light jog. Just as she was beginning to recover from her awkward confession, two bikini-clad blondes got on the stationary bikes that faced them.

"Okay now, that's just ridiculous. It's got to be against the rules to work out in just bikinis. It seems unsanitary."

Ace grinned, barely breaking a sweat. "I don't know. This is Vegas. I'm sure it's not the most shocking thing that's taken place in here."

Ronnie thought for a minute and a private smile crossed her face. "Yeah, I guess you're right."

"Wait a minute. I saw the look you just had on your face. What was that all about?"

"Nothing. I just remembered something. You're probably right."

"What did you remember?"

She shook her head. "It's not my story to tell."

"Then don't name names, but you have to spill it. Now."

She didn't need much prodding. Ronnie had never been able to resist a good piece of gossip. "Okay, back home, I knew someone that had a little after-hours workout in the gym that we belong to."

Ace was silent for a moment, then his eyes went wide. "Oh, no, are you telling me that Cara had sex in the gym?"

Ronnie almost lost her footing. "I never said it was Cara."

"I know you didn't. I'm just putting two and two together. She used to be a fitness trainer. She probably had keys to the place to sneak in and get busy on the bench-press machine or something."

"She'd kill me if she ever found out that you knew. You have to keep that to yourself."

Ace laughed. "No problem. I know how to keep a secret. I'm just shocked, really. I always thought she sounded like she was a bit…conservative."

"She was, but I guess she loosened up when she met her husband-to-be."

"Now tell me this, where's the freakiest place you've had sex?"

"That's a nosy question," she said, looking around to make sure no one was eavesdropping on them.

"You can say that to me after last night?"

"I can say that because I don't really have a good answer. I'm kind of a regular girl when it comes to that stuff. It's always been indoors and on a bed."

"Unbelievable. If I'd been laying odds on it, I would have bet you were the adventurous type."

"That's why it's a gamble," she said. "And you would've bet wrong." To take the attention away from herself, she asked, "What about you? Are you adventurous?"

He flashed all his teeth in a devilish smile. "Maybe."

"So? Are you going to tell me?"

He thought for a few seconds. "I guess I'd have to say the car wash."

"What?" Ronnie stopped running for a moment to stare at him.

"You know, the kind that lets you stay in the car while it drives itself through the brushes and sprays."

"Oh," she said, resuming her pace. "Wait a minute. Don't those car washes have big viewing windows where people can watch?"

"If anyone was watching, all they saw was me sitting in the driver's seat."

She stopped again. "I don't understand."

"Of course, my girlfriend was missing from view. I was getting a little wash and polish of my own."

"Oooh!" Blushing, Ronnie started running faster on the treadmill. Great. Now Ace probably thought she was boring.

After that, Ace tried to continue the conversation, but Ronnie kept increasing the pace until they were both panting too hard to talk.

When the timer sounded on her machine, she jumped off. "I'm going to hit the shower. So much to do today. See you in Kauai tomorrow."

"But, Ronnie, don't you want to— Okay, bye."

Ace shook his head as he watched Ronnie walk away while he tried to catch his breath. He always managed to push things to the point that she ran away. Everything had been going so well between them. Had he ruined it by sharing too much too soon?

For every two steps forward with Ronnie, Ace took one step back. Long-term relationships were foreign to him, and here he was pursuing one with a woman who might not be ready for it.

How could he even be sure that he was ready for it? He didn't exactly have a long track record with serious relationships. After watching the slow death of his parents' marriage, for a long time he hadn't even believed true love really existed.

But being with Ronnie felt really good. She told him this morning that they were just having fun. Maybe he had to stop focusing on getting serious and just concentrate on the fun.

Ace smiled to himself. Just because she hadn't been sexually adventurous in the past didn't mean they couldn't change that. An idea began to formulate for their date the next night in Kauai.

"Well, that's an evil grin if I ever saw one," Garett said, coming up next to him.

Ace laughed at his friend, who was better dressed for the tennis court than the gym, in his white polo and shorts. "I don't know what you're talking about."

"Oh, I think you do. Wasn't that Veronica I just saw leaving?"

"If you knew her at all, you'd know she hates to be called Veronica."

He shrugged. "She looks more like a Veronica than a Ronnie to me. So how was your date last night?"

"It went surprisingly well, considering that dirty trick you pulled."

"Dirty trick?" Garett said with feigned innocence. "I don't know of any dirty tricks. But you don't have to thank me for the tickets. Just knowing you're satisfied is thanks enough."

"Thank you? I should sock you. If Ronnie hadn't been such a good sport, you could have ruined everything."

"But I didn't, did I? Dare I ask where you slept last night?"

"You can dare, but you won't get an answer."

Garett laughed. "That's okay. I don't need an answer. I called your room several times this morning and you weren't there. So actually, I take it back. You really *should* thank me."

Ace rolled his eyes. Garett wasn't ever going to change and it was useless to try to reason with him. "Whatever. I have to go shower."

"Stop by the front desk on your way up to your room. I left a clipping for you."

Ace stopped in his tracks. "What kind of clipping?"

"I was able to work my magic and get you mentioned in the local paper. I wanted to get you in something national but it was short notice."

Feeling a tingle of suspicion sneak up his neck, Ace all but ran to the front desk. The woman behind the counter handed him an envelope, and Ace stepped on the elevator and pulled out the clipping.

It was a very small article but it carried a powerful impact.

The Sexy Chef Makes Good On His Name With Fellow Reality Show Contestant.

The article went on to describe their date and the racy show they'd attended last night. Suddenly sweat was pouring down his back that had nothing to do with his workout.

Hopefully, Ronnie would board her flight before anyone could show her the local paper, Ace thought, hastily stuffing the clipping back into the envelope. If she found out that this story had originated with his publicist, their romance really would be just a one-night stand.

Chapter 11

Ronnie boarded the plane feeling her usual preflight jitters, coupled with second thoughts about her night with Ace. It was time to admit that she'd gotten in over her head. She'd planned on merely dipping her toe into the dating pool. Instead, she'd done a cannonball straight into the deep end. It was time to get out before she drowned.

Ace was a great friend and an amazing chef. But their conversation at the gym reminded her that he was in a different league.

In school, when he'd been a big fish in a little pond, women had clamored to reel him in. Now that he was a big fish in a big pond, Ace was catch of the day on every girl's menu.

Ronnie knew she'd never be able to compete with the beautiful, experienced women Ace was used to dating. They'd had one incredible night together, but what if that was just an average night for him?

She didn't need that kind of pressure. Not when she had to shoulder the weight of moving up from behind in the next round of the *Food Fight*.

Trying to calm her frenetic thoughts, Ronnie settled into her roomy seat with a glass of wine, next to LQ.

"I guess you had a good time on your date last night," LQ said. "I thought you and Ace were just friends."

"What do you mean?" Had LQ somehow figured out that Ronnie had slept with Ace? Could LQ read it on Ronnie's face?

"I'm talking about the article in the *Vegas Review.*"

Ronnie's heart leaped. "We were mentioned in the *Vegas Review?*"

"You didn't see it? My husband saw it online and called to tell me about it. I assumed someone already told you. Here. I have a printout of it in my purse. They say no press is bad press."

Her adrenaline spiked. That didn't sound good.

Sure enough, there they were. A blush instantly crept up Ronnie's neck as she read the headline.

"So, you're dating the competition," LQ said, unable to hide the note of judgment in her voice. "I hope it's to throw him off his game and not the other way around."

Ronnie tightened up, not yet feeling the calming effects of the wine. "LQ, Ace and I are old friends. We respect each other too much to let anything personal get in the way of our work."

"I'm glad to hear that, because the Sexy Chef is a notorious player. I had a friend who—"

"Don't worry." Ronnie wasn't in the mood for a lecture. "I don't think Ace and I will have another night like last night. I'm not going to let a man steal my focus. If anything, my desire to beat him is stronger than ever."

"Good," LQ said, clearly relieved. "I need that prize

money to buy a new house. I'm not raising a family in that chichi Georgetown apartment we have now."

As embarrassing as it was to have her friend questioning her judgment, something else was bothering Ronnie. "I just can't believe such a small local paper cares anything about two chefs out on the town."

"Celebrity chefs. You're going to have to get used to this kind of thing from now on. Gourmet TV has a lot of viewers and food competitions get big ratings."

"I guess I didn't realize that." All the more reason to keep things strictly business with Ace. It was bad enough to make a mistake, but it was worse still to do it with the whole world watching.

The combination of white wine and not getting enough rest the night before put Ronnie to sleep shortly after the plane took off. She awoke sometime later at the plane's sudden lurching dip and a smattering of startled gasps. Disoriented, Ronnie looked at LQ, who was wide-eyed and gripping the armrest tightly.

The fasten seat belts sign dinged and the captain's voice came on over the loudspeaker. "We're flying into a thunderstorm and will be experiencing some heavy turbulence for the next several minutes. Please stay in your seats until I turn off the fasten seat belts sign. Flight attendants, please take your seats, as well."

Ronnie caught her breath. She was a reluctant flyer at best, at times like this she considered giving it up all together.

The plane continued to bob in the air, and Ronnie could hear the rain pummeling the aircraft. Swallowing hard, she couldn't help thinking that they might actually crash.

Throughout the plane she heard nervous laughter and several frightened shrieks with each jerk and dip. In the back of the plane, a baby was wailing inconsolably, and

Ronnie had to fight the urge to do the same. If she started screaming over a little turbulence, security might carry her off the plane when they landed in Hawaii.

Trying to keep her nerves in check, Ronnie closed her eyes and clutched the armrest. Where was that wine when she needed it? Of course, it would take an entire bottle to dull her anxiety right now.

That's when her worst fear was realized.

The oxygen masks dropped from their panel. Physically shaking, Ronnie reached for the mask, fumbling to fit it over her mouth.

LQ, mask over her mouth, was audibly praying and crossing herself. Ronnie decided it was time for her to do the same.

Aloud she said, "Dear God, please don't let this plane crash."

When her plane landed safely in Kauai, Ronnie had never been so happy to see the ground. LQ immediately pulled out her cell phone to call her husband. And Ronnie, who was just glad to be alive, was stuck in a daze as she went through the motions of claiming her baggage and picking up her rental car.

When she finally got into the convertible and started the drive to her hotel, her mood began to brighten. The scenery was like nothing she'd ever seen before. Where Las Vegas had been all lights and architectural whimsy, Kauai was flora and tropical fantasy.

As Ronnie drove toward her hotel, the sun was beginning to set over the mountains. On impulse, she pulled over and parked on the side of the road so she could take in the view. For those few minutes, though they'd seemed like hours, when the wind had batted the plane around like a kitten with a ball of yarn, Ronnie had thought she'd never see a sight like this one again.

As she watched the wind ripple through the palm trees, she realized something important. She was being foolish about Ace.

He'd made it clear that he wanted to be with her, and she really wanted to be with him. What else mattered?

She could continue to get hung up on his past, or she could enjoy the present. After that harrowing flight, she knew life was too short not to enjoy it.

Besides, Ace was nothing like any man she'd dated before. Looking back, she could see that there had been a dozen warning signs with men like Andre. She'd known Ace as a friend for so long, she already knew that he cared about her.

It was time to stop holding back and let herself enjoy being in a romance again. Enjoying the company of a handsome man didn't mean she had to be stupid about it. There wasn't anything wrong with a little competition fling. Once the *All-Star Food Fight* was over, they'd be returning to their old lives in separate states.

And letting herself trust Ace a little bit didn't mean she was blind to reality. As LQ had reminded her, he'd always been a bit of a player. He wasn't heartless, but he didn't stay with one woman for long. Because they were friends, Ronnie believed she was more than just another notch on his headboard. But that didn't mean he wouldn't eventually go looking for his next seduction.

If she entered the relationship with her eyes wide open for a change, maybe she could avoid getting hurt.

Ronnie got back into her car and drove to the Hyatt Regency Hotel in Poipu, where she was greeted with a cool drink and a Hawaiian lei.

As she entered the open-air hotel, she could hear the

blowing of a conch shell and a native drumbeat. Torches were being lit on the back of the property. Ronnie felt like she was stepping into another world.

This is a new beginning, she thought to herself. *I'm going to stop living like a fat girl.*

She hadn't lived like one when she *was* one, so why was she stifling herself now that she was thin? It was time to get reacquainted with the old Ronnie who had no worries or fears. What would *that* Ronnie do next? That was easy.

Go big, or go home!

Chapter 12

It was nearly noon when Ace pulled his rental car up to the hotel. He'd expected the bellhop to reach for his luggage, and he'd even expected a lei greeting.

But instead, as he walked toward the opening, three women dressed in hula skirts lined up to dance for him.

Instantly, his mouth curved with male appreciation as his gaze skimmed over the trio of shaking hips and swaying arms. "Now, this is what I call VIP treatment."

Traditional Hawaiian hula dancers—

Wait a minute. His eyes skidded back to the dancer in the middle. "Ronnie!" He clapped his hands together in surprise. "This is fantastic."

Like the two others, Ronnie was dressed in a grass skirt, a floral halter and a headpiece made from purple orchids. He watched her hips roll and sway with new appreciation. As her body moved, he saw the little stud in her navel glint in the sunlight.

The dancers circled him, and as they swayed by, they each put a lei over his head.

Ronnie gave him her lei last, leaning forward to kiss him on the cheek. Ace laughed out loud. "This is amazing."

She pulled away, looking embarrassed. "Oh my God, they're everywhere."

Ace looked over his shoulder and saw a photographer standing a few feet away, snapping pictures. This had to be Garett's doing. If his friend hadn't flown out last night, Ace would have had the chance to call off this media circus Garett was orchestrating.

"Don't worry, he probably works for the hotel," Ace said, trying to downplay the photographer's presence. "Someone will probably try to sell us a copy of that picture later today."

As soon as he got inside, he'd wring Garett's neck and make sure that picture never saw the light of day. Until then, he didn't want her to worry. "This is the best greeting I've ever gotten. How did you set this up?"

Ronnie's eyes were bright with mischief. "I took a hula lesson this morning. The girls teaching the class were so nice. They agreed to come out here and help me give you a special welcome."

Ace's heart was light in his chest. He'd left Las Vegas wondering if Ronnie was going to start pulling away. And here she was arranging this incredible surprise for him. Maybe she *did* share his feelings.

"LQ and I are going on a tour of the botanical gardens this afternoon, so I knew I wouldn't see you until dinner. This is just my way of saying hello."

Ace leaned down, circling her bare waist with his hands. "Well, hello," he said, pressing his lips against hers.

He knew he was giving the photographer a show, but

he was going to have to deal with that later. Right now he just wanted to feel Ronnie close to him.

He took his time, letting his lips sip at hers. Her lips parted slightly, and he teased the opening with his tongue. When the kiss finally broke, they were both out of breath.

Ronnie sighed. "I thought my hello was pretty good. But yours is better."

Ace was reluctant to let her go. "Dinner at eight?"

"Don't kid yourself, we're both from the East Coast, and there's a six-hour time difference. At eight o'clock we'll both be snoring. Let's make it six."

"Six it is. Meet me in the lobby. I'll take care of the rest."

After he and Ronnie parted ways, it took Ace a few minutes to check in. Then he called Garett to meet him for lunch. His friend showed up to the poolside grill without a clue as to how upset Ace was.

"We need to talk," he said as soon as Garett pulled up a chair.

"What's on your mind, buddy?"

"Did you sic a reporter on me this morning?"

Garett laughed, crossing his legs. "No, not at all."

Ace sank back into his chair in relief. "Thank God, because Ronnie set up an amazing hula greeting and—"

"He wasn't a reporter," Garett continued. "He's just a photographer I hired. I wasn't happy with the coverage we got in Vegas. I thought we could stimulate some national press if we leaked some juicy photos."

"Oh geez, it *was* you," Ace said, pounding the table with his fist. "I thought I told you to kill the whole showmance thing. I don't want photographers popping up every time I'm alone with Ronnie."

"That's what you think. But just that little article in the

Vegas Review has caused the preorders for your cookbook to go up on Amazon."

"Garett, I want to make this crystal clear. Fire the photographer you hired and kill the photos. If I see that shot of Ronnie kissing me in a hula skirt in a newspaper, you'll regret it."

Garett held up his hand as if he were swearing on the Bible. "Okay, fine. I promise to fire the photographer. You definitely won't see that photo in the paper, okay? Now, let's order. I'm starving."

"Thank you," Ace said, opening his menu. Now he could plan his romantic date without any worries.

At six o'clock Ronnie met Ace in the lobby as promised. Taking her new attitude to heart, she'd gone shopping after seeing the botanical gardens and bought several sexy new outfits.

Today she was wearing a white orchid-print sarong dress that knotted at her breasts, with a pair of high-heeled sandals. She wore her hair down with a white plumeria flower by her ear.

Ace, wearing his own bamboo-print Hawaiian shirt with tan slacks, took her arm. "You look perfect for what I have planned this evening."

He escorted her to his car and they drove toward the mountains.

Normally Ronnie didn't like to ride with the convertible top down. Her hair would whip around her face and she'd end up looking like a bedraggled mop by the time the ride was over. But this evening there was just enough breeze to blow through her curls without tousling them.

The late-spring air in Kauai was cool enough to be refreshing and warm enough to be comfortable. They were surrounded by breathtaking views at every turn. Colors seemed more brilliant in Kauai. The grass was a deep emerald, the flowers were bright enough to paint a rainbow and the sky framed it all in a dreamy blue.

"I feel like we're living in a fantasy right now. If we didn't have to compete in three days, I'd never want to leave."

"Fantasy is the theme for this date. For now, forget about the competition and everyone else. This evening is just for us."

"Where are we going?" She studied the smirk on his face. "You're not going to tell me, are you?"

"No, but I don't think you'll be disappointed."

They continued up the mountain, across tiny one-lane bridges and beside steep drop-offs. Ace pulled over a couple of times so they could enjoy the unexpected waterfalls trickling down the mountains, and chickens running wild on the side of the road.

Finally they pulled into the parking lot of a tiny building. Ronnie read the sign on the window. "Helicopter tours?"

"This is the best way to see Kauai. I came here once a few years ago, and the helicopter tour was the highlight of my visit."

Ronnie's heart started to race. "I didn't have a chance to mention this, but I had a really bad flight. I'm not sure I'm ready to get into another aircraft so soon. Especially one so small."

Ace came around to her side of the car and pulled her door open. She still wasn't convinced that she wanted to get out.

"Do you trust me?"

She took a deep breath. He'd never given her a reason not to. "Yes."

"Then know that I wouldn't put you in danger. This

company is the best. And I'll be right beside you to hold your hand. Believe me. You don't want to miss this."

Hadn't she decided to stop holding herself back? Even though the thought of getting in that tiny aircraft gave her the shakes, she couldn't give up flying. If she made it through this next *Food Fight* round, she'd have to fly to Paris. And even if she didn't, she'd still have to fly home. Now was her chance to lay her fears to rest.

"Okay, let's do it," she said, finally.

They entered the building, filled out their release forms, which did nothing to assuage her fears, and were escorted out to the helicopter.

They put on headphones so the pilot could speak to them above the noise of helicopter blades, and Ace took her hand. Ronnie held her breath as the helicopter lifted off. She soon forgot her reservations as she got caught up in the incredible sights below her.

They flew over the colorful fingers of Nā Pali Coast and over more waterfalls than she could count. The pilot pointed out the falls from the old TV show *Fantasy Island* and the movie *Jurassic Park*. Ace squeezed her hand as they looked down into the stunning gorge of Waimea Canyon.

Between the Hawaiian music the pilot played for ambience and his funny commentary, Ronnie realized that she was having the time of her life. And she would have missed it if she hadn't allowed herself to trust Ace.

After they'd been in the air for nearly an hour, Ronnie was shocked to see the helicopter descending in the middle of an open field. Immediately, her heart started hammering. "Is there something wrong with the helicopter? Why are we landing?"

"This is your final destination," the pilot said, and Ronnie looked at Ace in confusion.

He just smiled cryptically and helped her out of the helicopter. He led her through a path of trees that opened to a gorgeous lagoon where a table for two had been set up. It was surrounded by tiki torches and two covered platters sat at each place setting.

Ronnie felt her eyes welling with tears. No one had ever gone to this much effort for her. She was always the one who planned Valentine's Day and birthday surprises. She'd practically come to the decision that romance was something men only practiced in the movies.

Trying not to blubber like a fool, Ronnie wobbled in the grass on her heeled sandals. "Why don't you take those off," Ace said, kneeling to unfasten the straps for her.

As soon as his big hands touched her ankle, her knees almost buckled. It must have been her rush of emotion that overwhelmed her. Because suddenly Ronnie wanted Ace with a passion she'd never experienced before.

He took her arm and helped her get seated at the table. Finally she could trust her voice to speak. "This is the most romantic thing anyone's ever done for me. Thank you."

Ace smiled. "Believe me, Ronnie, you deserve it. It may not be my place to say this, but, I caught a glimpse of how Andre used to treat you, and it always bothered me. I want you to know that not all men are like that."

Feeling embarrassed, Ronnie stared at her covered platter. She knew the incident Ace was talking about.

A couple of years ago, she'd surprised Andre with a weekend in New York City. She took him to dinner at one of Ace's restaurants. When Ace had come to the table to greet them, instead of complimenting the food, Andre had joked about how a big girl like her could always be counted on to clear her plate.

She hadn't appreciated it at the time, but Ace had stared Andre down as if he wanted to punch him.

Not wanting to spoil the night with bad memories, she pushed that thought aside. "What's for dinner?"

Ace reached over and uncovered both dishes, revealing a grilled fish with a tropical salsa and steamed vegetables. It looked both healthy and delicious. "Taste it and you tell me."

Ronnie took a forkful of the fish and the salsa together. "Mmm, this tastes like mahimahi with a light herb and—" She tasted it again. "Macadamia nut crust?" Ronnie looked at him suspiciously. "You didn't make this, did you?"

"No, I didn't. I had it delivered. I told the chef to surprise me and make sure it was a local dish."

"Well, he outdid himself. This salsa is fantastic. I taste star fruit, mango and papaya."

"And there's a bit of citrus and lime. Maybe grape-fruit?"

They went back and forth throughout the meal picking out the ingredients and trying to guess the cooking methods of the dish.

Finally, Ace reached into a picnic basket under the table and pulled out their desserts. A giant slab of chocolate cake garnished with fresh fruit, and one fork.

Since their first date, Ronnie hadn't been as faithful to her diet as she'd wanted, but she promised herself that she'd make up for it later.

She couldn't pass up being fed the delectable chocolate dessert by her even more delectable chocolate date.

As Ace fed her the last bite, Ronnie's mind returned to her earlier amorous thoughts. "Did you say we're all alone out here?"

"Not a soul for miles."

Her back straightened. "Then how are we getting back to the hotel?"

"Don't worry about that until it's time. I've taken care

of everything. In fact, I thought you might want to take a dip in the lagoon."

"You should have told me. I would've brought my suit."

He grinned. "You don't need a suit. Besides, I'd do anything to keep you from putting on that frumpy black thing you call a bathing suit. I thought we could go skinny-dipping."

Ronnie frowned, almost starting to protest. But as she glanced at the inviting pool of water, her mind began to change. The sun was just beginning to set, casting the water with a vibrant pink glow. They were surrounded by lush trees blooming with tropical flowers from hibiscus to plumeria. She may never get this chance again. And with the setting sun and the cover of trees, she really *did* feel as though they were all alone in the world.

"I've never gone skinny-dipping before. But you might be able to talk me into it."

"You need some persuading?"

Before Ronnie could answer, Ace got out of his seat to pull her against him. Lowering his face to hers, he gave her a deep, stirring kiss.

"I'd love to make love to you surrounded by all of this beauty," he whispered.

Then he reached for the knot between her breasts that held her sarong together and let it fall to the ground. Underneath she wore a cream slip-dress, which quickly followed her sarong.

Ronnie unbuttoned Ace's Hawaiian shirt and shoved it off his shoulders. He helped push his slacks down over his large, muscular thighs.

By the time they were both nude, the last thing on Ronnie's mind was swimming. So when he lifted her into his arms, she stared into his eyes, anticipating the feel of his hands on her body.

Instead, his arms disappeared and she was falling. Cool water instantly surrounded her. With a flashback to the pool in Las Vegas, she surfaced, sputtering.

This time, Ace stayed close, pulling her against him with one hand, and wiping her face clear of water with the other.

Before she could say anything to kill the mood, his lips were on hers again. Moments ago the water had been a shocking cold. Now, with their bodies pressed together, they could have made it boil.

Ace's dark, wet skin shone like polished onyx. Ronnie felt like the luckiest woman in the world to have such a handsome hunk all to herself.

Instead of Frank Sinatra on the stereo, they had the night sounds of birds and insects chittering their mood music. Instead of candlelight they had the amber glow of the setting sun. There were no bedsheets to drape their bodies—instead they were blanketed in teal-blue water and evening mist.

As they kissed, Ronnie could feel Ace's arousal. She would finally have a romantic adventure to file away in her memories. She was fulfilling a fantasy she didn't even know she'd had.

With strong arms, Ace began to lift her out of the water, and her legs instinctively encircled his waist. It was exciting to have a man burly enough to hold her without complaint. With Ace, she felt like the most delicate flower.

Though her eyes were closed, she sensed a flash of light. Her eyes snapped open. "Was that lightning?"

Ace's eyes were hooded and distracted. "What do you mean?"

"I saw a flash of—there it is again." This time she could

see it was coming from the trees. And it was followed by several more.

Ace lowered her into the water. "It's a camera."

Immediately Ronnie sank into the water up to her neck. "Someone's watching us?" She remembered the article in the *Las Vegas Review*. Maybe that photographer at the hotel had been with the paparazzi, too. "Oh, no!"

"Stay down," Ace ordered in a no-nonsense tone. Then he charged out of the water, barely pausing to grab his pants.

Ronnie huddled in the water, hoping it was dark enough to hide her body. Ace, as bold as ever, ran for the trees while pulling on his pants.

She saw more flashes and heard some shouting before Ace reappeared. Grabbing a towel from under their table, he stood with open arms, motioning to her that it was safe to leave the water.

Starting to shiver with both chill and adrenaline, Ronnie skittered into Ace's arms, where he wrapped the towel around her and helped her dress.

"What happened?" She bent over to slip on her shoes.

"It seems a reporter showed up to photograph us," he answered tersely, his brows knit in anger.

Ronnie shook her head. "Are you kidding me? Are Brad and Angelina in the area? Because I can't imagine why the paparazzi would care about a couple of chefs. Especially when they would have had to go to such lengths to find us out here."

Ace looked tense. "You're right. This shouldn't have happened," he said, vehemently.

Ronnie still couldn't wrap her mind around it. "I don't mean to sound skeptical, because I know you're popular with your fans. But are you really so famous that the paparazzi stalk you?"

With them both fully dressed now, Ace wrapped his arms around her shoulders and started guiding her out of the clearing. "No, I'm not. And I never wanted to be. I'm going to have to find a way to put a stop to this."

Ronnie saw that they were approaching the main road where a limo was waiting. She had to admit that she was relieved not to be getting into a helicopter again. Looking at Ace's profile, he seemed genuinely upset.

She squeezed his shoulder before climbing into the limo. "I'm sorry your romantic evening was interrupted, but all is not lost. We can finish what we started back at the hotel."

He climbed in beside her. "This is all my fault. I don't know what kind of pictures that photographer got, but I'll do whatever I can to make sure they don't make it into the paper."

Ronnie laughed. "Could it be that they got a bogus tip? Maybe they thought we were Beyoncé and Jay-Z."

Ace just shook his head, refusing to pick up her light mood. She wasn't thrilled about their romantic tryst getting interrupted by a photographer. And if she really took the time to think about it, she'd be mortified. But Ace was taking it harder.

She could only imagine the time and money he'd spent trying to make the evening special for her. Obviously he felt that everything was ruined now. Apparently, it would be up to her to salvage the night.

In the lobby, Ronnie tugged on Ace's arm. "Come back to my room with me. I think I know how to cheer you up."

He gave her hand a squeeze as he pulled away. "Not tonight. I have a headache."

She laughed. "Are you a suburban housewife now? 'Not tonight, I have a headache'?"

He shook his head. "Seriously, I think I'm just going to take some aspirin and go to sleep. I'll see you tomorrow."

Disappointed, Ronnie went back to her room. Too wired to go to sleep, she dialed LQ's cell phone. "What are you up to?"

LQ yawned. "I was getting ready for bed. I thought you'd be doing the same. I stopped by your room earlier, but you didn't answer."

Ronnie sighed. LQ would think she was nuts after their conversation on the plane yesterday, but LQ was bound to find out eventually that Ronnie was still dating Ace. "I had a date. With Ace."

There was a long pause. "Really? But, what about—"

"I know what you're thinking, but the time we're spending together has nothing to do with the competition. He's a great guy, and I think I deserve to be with a great guy for a change."

"How can you be sure he's as great as you think he is?"

"He planned the most romantic date for us tonight." Ronnie told LQ about the helicopter tour and gourmet meal beside the lagoon. "It would have been perfect if those crazy paparazzi photographers hadn't interrupted us."

LQ sighed heavily. "Ronnie, this just doesn't sound right to me. How do you know that Ace didn't set this whole thing up for publicity?"

Ronnie scoffed. "If you'd seen how angry Ace was, you wouldn't even question it."

"That could be an act. I tried to tell you before. One of my girlfriends who used to model in New York used to date Ace. She had a really bad experience."

Ronnie stiffened. "What happened?"

"She said he used her to get free publicity for his

restaurant. He took advantage of her rising fame. They were photographed together all over town, then after his big opening, he dumped her."

"Come on, LQ. That doesn't sound like Ace at all. I'm sure your friend misunderstood the reason for their breakup. He doesn't need to use cheap tricks like that. His food speaks for itself."

"Fine, it's your life. You can believe what you want. But I'd be careful if I were you."

Ronnie hung up the phone feeling sick to her stomach. Was it true? Could Ace be responsible for the press suddenly taking an interest in the two of them?

She remembered his miserable expression on the limo ride home. There was no way he was faking that. Getting to her feet, Ronnie pushed LQ's words aside. Ace was so distraught over how the evening had ended he'd given himself a headache. She shouldn't have let him go back to his room alone.

Smiling to herself, she went to her closet. It wasn't too late for her to nurse him back to health.

Chapter 13

Walking back to his room, Ace knew he hadn't been good company. But he just couldn't let his anger go. Garett had gone too far. Hadn't he made it clear that he didn't want to turn his relationship with Ronnie into a media spectacle?

Even though he'd rather be with Ronnie, he wouldn't be able to focus on romance until he found Garett and tore him a new one. He'd gone to great lengths to win Ronnie's trust and make the evening one she'd never forget. Now, once again, Garett's schemes could ruin everything.

If nude photos of them frolicking in the lagoon showed up in the morning paper, how could he ever look Ronnie in the eye again? Garett was responsible for this and he worked for Ace. She'd never believe that Ace hadn't put him up to it.

What made things worse was that he hadn't told anyone his plans. Especially not Garett.

Sure, Garett had been known to ignore his wishes in the

past, but only on trivial matters. They'd been friends for many years, but if Ace couldn't get through to him, he'd have to fire him.

Ace paced his room, dialing Garett's number on his cell phone every two minutes. The coward wouldn't answer. He probably had his ringer turned off.

He decided to call the front desk to connect him to Garett's room. Even if he wasn't there now, he'd have to show up at some point. And Ace would ring the line every two minutes. If Garett wanted to sleep that night, he'd have to talk to Ace first.

Before he could hit the keypad, there was a knock at his door. Ace dropped the phone and stalked to the door. Maybe Garett had realized Ace was trying to reach him and had decided to face the music in person.

When Ace jerked open the door, he got a surprise.

Ronnie was smiling at him from the hallway, holding a large banana split.

Mouth agape, Ace just stood there with the door open. She squeezed past him into his room.

"Shut the door, Ace. I want to show you something." She was wearing a short lavender raincoat and her high-heeled sandals. It wasn't raining.

Unable to form words, he did as he was told.

She put the sundae on the table. Untying her belt, Ronnie pulled open the raincoat to reveal a simple black bra and panties. "I thought you needed something sweet to make you feel better."

Her honey-colored skin looked tasty enough to eat. He took a step toward her, and she dropped the raincoat on the floor and picked up the sundae.

"I know what I said about food in the bedroom, but I thought you might be able to change my mind." Ronnie took a cherry and placed it between her glossy lips. Then she crooked her finger for him to come and get it.

Still unable to speak, Ace just nodded. Leaning over, he sucked the cherry from her lips into his mouth. He ate the cherry, tasting the sweet juice and her soft lips all at once.

Ronnie led him over to the bed, pushed him down and began taking off his clothes. "Do you still need an aspirin?"

Ace dipped his finger first into the hot fudge and then into her cleavage. "No, I think I found my cure," he said, leaning forward to lick the fudge away.

Still on East Coast time, Ace woke up at 6:00 a.m. to find Ronnie staring at him. "You're already awake," he whispered, realizing his voice was a bit hoarse.

"Yes, I've been awake since five thirty. Jet lag, I guess."

"Good. Since we're both awake, why don't we have breakfast in the hotel restaurant overlooking the ocean?"

Ronnie levered herself up on one arm. "I don't know. Do you think it's safe to be seen together? Now I feel like there are photographers hiding in every bush. We've already had one article in the paper and there might be another one today." She cringed.

Ace's stomach turned over. For a short while, he'd been able to forget about the paparazzi. Ronnie's surprise seduction had cleared his mind of everything but her.

But, he hadn't caught up with Garett yet, which meant anything could happen today. He had to get through to him before things got further out of control.

Trying to downplay how much it still bothered him, Ace said, "I'm offended that you're ashamed to be seen with me.

But, if it will put your mind at ease, we could always order room service. My balcony overlooks the ocean, too."

"That's not a bad idea. I'm starving."

After breakfast in Ace's room, Ronnie allowed him to talk her into going down to the beach for a surfing lesson. So she went back to her room to change and promised to meet him on the beach.

Even though staying in had felt a bit like hiding out, Ronnie preferred to think of it in a more romantic light. They weren't sneaking around. They were having a clandestine rendezvous.

Donning her standard black tank suit, Ronnie threw a T-shirt and shorts on top of it. Then she heard a knock at her door.

"LQ, what are you—"

Her friend bounded into the room with her laptop under her arm. "Where have you been all morning? I got something important to show you."

Ronnie felt heat creeping up her neck. "I was— Last night I—"

LQ held up a hand to halt Ronnie's stammering. "Don't say any more. I can guess."

She set up her laptop on the bed and flipped open the screen. "These pictures showed up online this morning."

Ronnie leaned forward, then clasped her hands to her face. A well-known gossip website had two pictures of Ronnie and Ace. One had been taken in front of the hotel yesterday when she was kissing him on the cheek in her hula outfit. The other was dark and blurry, but it was two people standing in a lagoon kissing.

Thankfully, it was impossible to make out who the two people were, but the gossip columnist speculated that it was Ronnie and Ace.

"I can't believe this is happening," Ronnie said, sinking to her knees in front of the computer.

LQ had her hand on her hip and was shaking her head. "I warned you this could happen. I still think Ace has the most to gain in this situation."

Ronnie shook her head. "No, he's as unhappy about this as I am. It's not his fault the press have glommed on to this story. He—"

She was interrupted by a knock at the door. It was a member of the hotel staff holding a bag from the gift shop.

"What's this?" she asked him.

The man smiled at her. "It's a gift courtesy of Ace Brown."

After closing the door, Ronnie dug into the bag. Her fingers connected with some fabric and string. Pulling her hand out of the bag, she found herself holding a tiny bikini.

LQ rolled her eyes. "You see? He's dressing you again."

Ronnie narrowed her eyes at her friend. "What are you talking about?"

"He took you shopping for a sexy dress in Las Vegas and then suddenly you show up in a newspaper article wearing it. Now there are photos of you half-naked online. If you put on that bikini, where do you think those photos will show up?"

"I think you're giving Ace too much credit. He doesn't think that far ahead. Elaborate schemes really aren't his style. I've been friends with him for many years, and I know he wouldn't—"

Exasperated, LQ cut her off. "Ronnie, do you really think he'd be dating you if you were still fat?"

Ronnie froze and so did LQ.

Her friend's face went pale as she realized she'd crossed a line. "Ronnie, I didn't mean to—"

"Actually, LQ, I have to go. I'm supposed to meet Ace on the beach." She crossed to the door and held it open for LQ.

Looking miserable, LQ left without another world.

Later, on the beach with Ace, Ronnie decided to block out all the stress of the morning. She didn't mention the photos to Ace because she knew the news would upset him. And for a little while, Ronnie just wanted to enjoy herself.

The surfing lesson was more fun that Ronnie ever would have anticipated. During the last thirty years of her life, no one ever would have accused her of being athletic. But the last several months in the gym had changed that.

She turned out to be a much better surfer than Ace, who kept wiping out in the waves.

"You're top-heavy," Ronnie called as he finally surfaced after another brutal fall. "For once all those big muscles are working against you."

He glared at her, clearing the water from his eyes. "I'm done with this," he said, heading for the beach.

Ronnie followed him, dropping her board in the sand beside his. "Honey, don't be such a sore loser. This should be good practice for the next *Food Fight*. You're going down hard."

"Such big talk for fourth place. You've got a lot of ground to make up. You might want to save face and focus on not getting sent home."

Pursing her lips, Ronnie struggled not to stoop to name-calling. "You'll see," she finally retorted.

After drying off and changing, they headed to the

hotel grill to share some overpriced hamburgers by the exotic pool.

"I wish they'd let me in that kitchen. I could really hook this burger up. A little asiago cheese and some cayenne pepper. You've never had a better burger."

Ace frowned at her. "Is everything a competition with you? Now you've got to show up the poor fry cook at the grill? Why don't you relax and save your energy for the real competition. Enjoy letting someone else cook for you."

She shrugged. "I do enjoy it. But don't you ever eat a meal and think, 'this food would be perfect if it just had…'"

"Only if it's a bad meal," he said, laughing. "This is a perfectly good hamburger. Stop talking and eat it."

Ronnie stuck her tongue out at him and took another bite.

He winked at her. "Don't show me your tongue unless you're going to come over here and put it to good use."

"Fine, I'll be quiet. But first there's something I've always wanted to know about you."

"And what is that?" Ace asked, wiping his hands on his napkin.

"Why did you become a chef? You're clearly athletic and you've always had a lot of hobbies. You could have done anything you wanted. Why cook?"

"It's a calling. I've always been a natural cook. Putting flavors together until they pop. That's what gives me satisfaction."

The words rolled out of his mouth almost without any thought.

Ronnie groaned. "No. That's your slick TV response. I've heard you say almost those exact words a thousand times. What's the real reason?"

Ace wadded up the napkin and dropped it on his plate. "You don't want to know the real reason."

"Yes, I do. Are you afraid to tell me?"

He shrugged. "I'm not afraid to talk about it. It's just not the cute story that makes good TV. That's why I've never told it to anyone before."

Ronnie hesitated. She hadn't meant to push him into uncomfortable territory. She was just about to let him off the hook when he began to speak.

"Cooking was the only way I could get my parents to stay in the same room."

"What do you mean? They're divorced, aren't they?"

"Now they are. But they stayed together for years, even though they could barely tolerate each other."

"So, where did the cooking come in?"

"When I was fourteen, we learned to make coq au vin in home economics. I came home and made a big production of making it for them. They sat through the meal for my benefit and even managed some small talk. That's when I convinced myself that I could make them love each other again, if I could keep them in the same room long enough."

Ronnie put her hand to her chest, feeling a deep sympathy for the teenager who felt responsible for keeping his parents together.

"I went through every cookbook in the house looking for romantic-sounding dishes. I made beef Wellington, chicken cordon bleu, and eventually, I even learned to make a crown roast of lamb."

"Did it work at the time?" Ronnie asked, knowing how the story eventually ended.

Ace shook his head, and Ronnie could see there was some lingering pain in his eyes. "No, only a kid would think romantic meals could unite two people who'd given up on their marriage years ago. They sat through the first few dinners but, after a while, I think they caught on to my plan. Suddenly my dad had to 'work late' several nights a week."

Ronnie touched his hand. "Maybe his workload *had* picked up."

"Yeah." Ace laughed, bitterly. "A few months later I found out that his workload's name was Sabrina."

"Oh, no!"

"Don't feel bad," Ace said, waving off her sympathy. "Turns out my little sister and I were much happier once our parents got divorced. It was the strain of their pretending that made everyone miserable. Plus, I discovered that I really do love cooking."

"Wow, that's some story." Ronnie sighed. "I'm sorry I made you go into it."

"It's okay. It doesn't hurt anymore, and both of my parents are happily married to other people."

"Oh, your dad married Sabrina?"

"Yeah. And Amber and Kelly. Turns out he's not so good with commitments."

Then Ace's cell phone rang, but he didn't move to answer it.

"Do you need to get that?"

He pulled out the phone and looked at the screen. "No. It's just Garett. I'll talk to him later. The conversation we need to have may take a while."

"Oh, if you have business—"

He shoved the phone back into his pocket. "No, I'd rather be here with you. The competition starts tomorrow, and we'll have to retreat to our respective corners. For now, I just want to enjoy our time together."

Ronnie felt herself warm. Ace wasn't holding anything back. He seemed genuinely into her. Maybe after the competition, there would be a chance for them to have something more serious.

She blinked as LQ's stinging words hit her again. *Do you really think he'd be dating you if you were still fat?*

Her skin lost its warmth. Was she falling back into her old ways? Here she was eating a hamburger instead of something healthy. Was she slacking on her common sense the way she'd been slacking on her diet?

When LQ had told Ronnie about her model friend's experience with Ace, Ronnie had defended him. When LQ accused Ace of leaking photos to the press, she'd defended him. The last time she'd defended a man against the concerns of her friends, she'd made a fool of herself. What if she just wasn't able to make smart judgments when it came to men?

Should she guard her heart? After what Ace had just told her about his parents, it was quite possible that he wasn't any better at commitments than his father. Or should she take a chance? His story also told her that he was a romantic. He focused on cooking for lovers because, once upon a time, he'd tried to rekindle his parents' love.

"So, now are you going to tell me what made you become a chef?" Ace asked, breaking into her heavy thoughts.

Ronnie laughed, relieved to let go of her worries until another time. "You already know the reason.… I cook because I like food."

Ace shook his head. "No chef worth his salt doesn't like to eat."

"You don't understand. It's not about liking to eat. It's about the food. The smells, the textures, the combination of flavors… I love all of it. Do you know how excited I can get over a basket of fresh strawberries or a cut of pork loin? When I see really good ingredients, my skin tingles. The possibilities are endless."

"I see." Ace smiled, leaning forward. "Fresh food is to Ronnie as a palette of paint is to an artist."

"I guess that's right," Ronnie said. "That's why winning this *Food Fight* is so important to me. It's an opportunity to realize a dream. If I win this, I can open another restaurant, and share my food with more people. When I was a kid, my mother, grandmother and I used to spend all day Sunday cooking. We'd bake fresh biscuits with honey, shell peas, batter and fry chicken with gravy…."

Ace closed his eyes. "Stop it. You're making me hungry all over again."

She laughed. "I know you're thinking the best part of the day was eating it all. But, believe it or not, the best part was the three of us talking and cooking in the kitchen all day. Those are some of the best memories of my life."

With those words, a memory hit her at once. Her father had disappeared on them when she was only eight, and she'd never met her grandfather. A lot of those talks over a hot stove had revolved around their troubles with men.

Ronnie swallowed hard. Until recently, she'd been repeating the pattern that her mother and grandmother had started. No wonder she always picked the wrong man. She'd been trained to think that was how it was supposed to be.

"You just got really quiet on me. Are you okay?"

Ronnie brought herself back into the moment. "Yes, I was just thinking how much I learned during those cooking sessions." Looking away, she added, "The tricky part now is not allowing my relationship with food to affect my clothing size."

"Trust me, Ronnie, you look good no matter what size you wear."

She felt her smile fade a bit. It was a nice line. But unfortunately, she knew it was nothing more than that.

Smooth talkers like Ace always knew the right thing to say, but she didn't need pretty lies.

The one thing she still believed was that men lied. They'd lied to her grandmother, they'd lied to her mother and they'd certainly lied to her. Ace might seem different on the surface, but she knew his flattery, however harmless, was still just a lie. After all, Ace hadn't been interested when she'd worn a larger size.

"I don't know about you, but this time in the sun has made me tired. I think I'll go upstairs for a nap."

Ace raised a wicked brow. "Care for some company?"

"No, thanks. Because of all your *company,* I haven't had a decent night's rest in days."

He leaned back in his chair. "I can't argue with that. You definitely need your rest. Tomorrow we duke it out."

Ronnie nodded. "Yeah, I want to get up early and check my kitchen setup. I don't want to have the same problems I had in Las Vegas."

Ace shook his head. "I don't think we're getting full kitchens."

She frowned. "What do you mean?"

"I mean that our stations will probably be set up outside. Think about it. The Hawaiian scenery will make a great backdrop, and I don't think this hotel has the indoor space we'd need. My guess is that we'll be set up in the same area as tonight's luau. The crew wouldn't even have to change much, since it will already be decorated."

Ronnie chewed her lip. That made a lot of sense. In fact, it was such a clever deduction, she wasn't quite sure why he was willing to share the information. A chef prepared to cook outside in the heat would strategize differently than one who expected to cook in an air-conditioned building.

"You're probably right. If you'd kept that theory to yourself, you could have had a big advantage over me."

Ace shrugged. "I guess so. But, you're a good chef. That kind of an edge wouldn't have helped me much. I plan to bring my A game, and I know you will, too."

Just as quickly as the dark cloud had settled over her thoughts, Ace had brought on the sunshine. She really wanted to trust him. And he was giving her reason after reason to give him a chance.

"If you're going to take a nap, I guess I'll go back to my room and do the same. You're going to be my date for the luau tonight, aren't you?"

His smile was so engaging. Ronnie had to remind herself not to let her heart get carried away. When the competition was over, they'd have to go back to their old lives. But for now, they were still having fun.

"Absolutely. I'm looking forward to it."

Ace laughed and clapped his hands as two hula dancers led Ronnie and several other audience members to the stage to dance with them.

She looked stunning in her pink sundress and lei of purple orchids. Again she wore her hair long and curly, framing her lovely face.

The drummers started a rousing, rhythmic beat, and Ronnie began to copy the hip shaking of the other hula dancers. Ace stared with appreciation as she moved her voluptuous curves in time to the beat. He felt like she was giving him a private show that he'd be sure to have her repeat when they were alone.

Even though they were supposed to get a good night's sleep before the next *Food Fight* round, Ace was determined to convince her to spend the night in his bed anyway. These last couple of days had been better than he could have imagined. He just hoped they both made it through tomorrow, so their time wouldn't come to an end.

Minutes later, Ronnie returned to the table beaming and out of breath. "That was so much fun. I'm going to have to teach those moves to Cara when I get home. Maybe I can convince her that hula is a better workout than the treadmill. Lord knows I hate that machine."

"You're welcome to hula for me anytime. You're a natural. And I love to watch those hips shake."

She threw her napkin at him. "Behave yourself, now."

Ace felt a buzzing in his shorts pocket. Pulling out his cell phone, he saw a text from Garett: BEEN LOOKING 4 U ALL DAY. WHAT TABLE R U AT? WILL COME OVER.

He felt his adrenaline spike. He'd been having such a good time, he'd almost managed to forget the paparazzi drama. He'd tried to call Garett again before the luau but hadn't had any luck. He couldn't speak to Garett now, in front of Ronnie. But Ace needed a chance to find out what was going on with these lame publicity stunts.

Ace typed: NEED 2 TALK. MY ROOM 5 MINS.

Ronnie leaned forward. "What are you doing?"

He pushed his chair back. "I have to run to my room for a minute. I'll be right back."

She gave him a puzzled look. "You have to go right now?"

"I won't be long," he said, getting up.

"Oh…okay."

Ace jogged back into the hotel, hating that he felt like he was up to no good. At least he could clear the air with Ronnie after he set Garett straight.

As soon as Ace rounded the corner and headed down the corridor toward his room, he saw Garett was already waiting outside.

"You have got to be the toughest guy to reach today. I woke up to a ton of messages from you this morning, but when I tried to return your calls, you wouldn't pick up."

"I was with Ronnie all day. And I didn't want to chew you out in front of her. Especially since your little stunt with the photographers last night almost ruined everything. Didn't I tell you to call off the press?"

"I did, but this thing has taken on a life of its own. Thanks to those steamy lagoon shots, your showmance with Ronnie is starting to generate some real interest. I have six calls from news outlets wanting quotes or an interview with you."

"You've got to put a stop to this. If Ronnie finds out you were behind this—"

"Look. The showmance angle is boosting the buzz about your cookbook. I don't see how Ronnie can object. She was a virtual nobody before this."

Ace rubbed his temples. "I don't think she's going to see it that way."

He gestured toward the door. "Are we going to go into your suite or not?"

"No, I don't even have time to get into this with you right now. Ronnie is waiting for me at the luau. I just need you to make all of this go away."

"No can do, buddy. This is a speeding train. All I did was start the engine, it has a destination all its own."

"Garett, this isn't over. I have to get back to Ronnie, but I'm not done talking about this."

"Relax. Just because the focus is on you and Ronnie right now doesn't mean that you're stuck with her. It's not going to interfere with you dating other women."

Ace released an exasperated sigh. "You're a piece of work, you know that?" he said, heading back down the hall.

Hearing Garett and Ace's voices coming closer, Ronnie ran back to the elevator. Fortunately, a family of four was just getting out, and she could jump in and jab the door-close button.

When she was safe behind the metal doors and the elevator was headed down to her floor, she let her face fall into her hands. A showmance?

Her fling with Ace had just been a publicity stunt planned by his publicist? LQ had tried to tell her Ace was responsible for the paparazzi shots, and Ronnie had defended him. She never would have known what was really going on if she hadn't gone to his room to tell him the luau was over.

Feeling tears welling in her eyes, Ronnie got off the elevator and walked liked a zombie back to her room. She thought she'd finally stopped playing the fool.

Turned out she was wrong.

Chapter 14

Ronnie sat on her bed staring at the carpet for several minutes. Tears made hot trails down her cheeks until they dripped off her chin. Leaning over, she watched them fall to the floor. Then she began to get angry.

Here she was crying over a man yet again. As always, the signs had been there and she'd ignored them. She'd also convinced herself that if she kept things light and fun, no man could hurt her. Wrong again.

As she always did when things like this happened, Ronnie picked up her cell phone and dialed Cara's number. After several rings she heard a groggy "Hello?"

Not picking up on her friend's sleepy voice, Ronnie said, "It happened again," without preamble.

"Before I ask you what happened, I just want to make sure you know that it's three a.m. here."

Ronnie's eyes went wide and she smacked her forehead. "Oh, no! I'm so sorry. Go back to bed." Embarrassed, she hung up the phone.

Seconds later, her cell phone rang. "Ronnie, I'm awake now. Tell me what happened."

"Do you think they need chefs in convents? Because I think the safest place for me is an environment without men."

"What happened with Ace? I just saw a story about the two of you on the entertainment news channel. It looked like you two were getting along great."

"Well, that news story is the problem. He and his publicist cooked up a plan to start a showmance with me so they could get extra press for his new cookbook."

"Wait a minute... He told you this?"

"No, I overheard them." Ronnie told Cara how she'd left the luau to find Ace and heard him talking with Garett.

Cara was quiet for a moment. "I don't believe it. Ace is a great guy. You know him. Are you sure he was in on the plan? Maybe his publicist realized the two of you were dating and took it upon himself to capitalize on that fact."

"That's not how it sounded. I heard Garett say he told Ace to get involved with me. Then he had to reassure him that he wasn't stuck with me if Ace wanted to date other girls."

"It's hard to believe Ace would go along with this. Have you talked to him?"

"No, and I don't plan to. LQ tried to warn me. She said he did something similar to a model friend of hers. But like you, I couldn't believe he'd stoop that low."

Cara sighed heavily. "Wow. Are you going to be okay, Ronnie?"

She lifted her chin. "Yes. Tomorrow is round two of the *Food Fight*. Now I don't just want to beat him. I need to. I have to show him that he can't hurt me."

"Good for you. Don't let this stand in the way of your

goals. For what it's worth, Ronnie, you shouldn't beat yourself up over this. Nobody could have anticipated this. It doesn't mean you'll never find true love."

Ronnie shook her head bitterly. "I'm glad you found it, Cara, but I'm starting to realize that it may not be for everyone. The women in my family seem to be magnets for the wrong men. We seem to do much better when we give up and go it alone."

She could tell her friend wanted to talk about it further, but Ronnie had wasted enough time thinking about Ace. From here on out, it was about winning and nothing else.

The morning of the competition, all the chefs were herded to an outdoor canopy where they would be told the terms of the second round. Just as Ace had suspected, they were going to be cooking outside in the tropical sun all day.

When he spotted Ronnie, he immediately rushed to her side. He'd been trying to reach her since the night before. She'd disappeared from the luau and hadn't answered her phone. Finally, Ace had decided she'd gotten tired and had gone to sleep early to rest for today's competition.

"There you are. I couldn't find you last night," he said, greeting Ronnie with a smile.

"I went to bed early," she said coldly, without looking up at him.

Puzzled, his eyes strayed to LQ who glared in his direction.

"That's what I figured. I'm sorry if I disappeared for too long," he said, wondering if she'd gotten upset when he'd left so suddenly. "I did come back to look for you. I at least wanted to tell you good-night."

Ronnie shrugged without looking at him, clearly indifferent to his presence. Ace bristled. He knew she'd be in the zone today, but did she have to act like he didn't exist? Ace stared in disbelief at her profile, but there really wasn't anything more to say. The host announced that they'd be getting started soon, and he had to join Marcel.

"Okay, well, good luck today."

Ronnie finally raised her eyes to meet his, and they were as cold as shards of ice. "I won't need it. But you will."

Ace almost physically shivered. Muttering under his breath, he crossed over to Marcel. His sous chef, picking up the vibe said, "Did you two have a falling out or does she just have her game face on?"

Ace sighed. "I don't know, but I can't worry about it. It's all about the food now."

The show's host took his mark, and the producer cued the camera operators. To Ace's surprise, the host was going to tell them the day's challenge on camera.

"Welcome to round two of the *All-Star Food Fight* here on Gourmet TV. In just a few minutes we're going to release our remaining competitors to their workstations to prepare a tropical feast."

Ace watched the monitor and saw the camera pan to four kitchen setups on the grounds where soon the afternoon sun would be beating directly down on them.

"The catch is that each chef is going to have three mystery ingredients that are popular in Hawaii that they *must* use in their dishes," the host continued. "One will be a protein, one will be produce and the final ingredient will be a spice. And to make sure we're taking things to the next level, each contestant is responsible for providing a carved fruit centerpiece to help showcase their dish."

Ace smacked Marcel on the back. The fruit sculpture was the only part of the challenge they'd been made aware of ahead of time. Marcel would be in charge of that section of the contest while Ace focused on the main course. He couldn't wait to find out what his ingredients would be. As soon as he saw them, he'd have to work fast to compose a winning dish.

The rest of the host's spiel was standard to the other *Food Fights* Ace had participated in. The host introduced the judges and talked about how they'd be scoring based on taste, presentation and originality.

"Okay, chefs. You will have one hour to complete your tropical feast for the judges, and your time begins now."

Four teams of chefs began running across the lawn. Ace got to his kitchen first and found a giant box sitting on his cutting board.

Pulling the lid off the box, he began to unload it. His first ingredient was a large portion of ahi tuna. A smile overtook his face right away. In preparation for this round of the competition, he'd been studying Hawaiian cuisine, and there were more than a few mentions of ahi tuna. Several dishes came to mind.

The next thing out of the box was jicama, a root vegetable with a creamy white interior similar to a potato. Ace nodded, thinking things were off to a great start.

Reaching down into the box he pulled out a pork loin. Confused, he studied it for several minutes. He turned to Marcel who was already gathering fruit from the shared pantry for his sculpture. "I thought we were only getting one protein."

Marcel shrugged, already concentrating on his task.

Then he saw the cameras running from Etta's station, where they'd been watching her unpack her box, to Ronnie's station next to Ace's. He looked over and saw her waving the judges to her workspace.

"I have no protein. Instead I have taro, wasabi and huli-huli sauce. Produce and two spices."

Hearing that, Ace figured it was a good time for him

to speak up. "There must have been some mix-up with the boxes. I have two proteins and no spice. Should we swap?"

Ace caught Ronnie's eye and she glared at him. He splayed his hands palm up to her, trying to communicate that he'd had nothing to do with it. But she just averted her eyes while the judges huddled to make a decision.

After visiting all the kitchens, the judges determined that Ace's and Ronnie's boxes were the only ones that were mixed up. The judges and the two chefs involved gathered in front of their workstations.

"How do you want to decide which ingredients go to which chef?" the host asked.

"Let's just make it easy," Ace volunteered. "Ronnie can choose which protein she wants and which spice to give me."

One of the judges, Chef Lomi, frowned at Ace. "Are you sure you want to put your fate in your competitor's hands?"

"Yeah, it's no problem. We just need to get this resolved so we can get back to our kitchens and start cooking."

He was also hoping that by taking the high road, he'd get Ronnie to stop glaring at him. It was one thing to take the competition seriously, but it was another thing to make it into an all-out war.

"Fine," Ronnie said, showing no signs of lightening up. "I want the ahi and he can have the wasabi."

Ace's heart sank. It wasn't until she took the tuna that he realized how much he'd wanted it. He could have made an amazing ahi poke. The raw-fish salad was a delicacy in Hawaii and would have been light and refreshing on such a hot day. But they'd lost so much time already that Ace didn't have the luxury to mourn his loss. Instead he had to regroup quickly and try to make a decent dish out of his jicama, pork and wasabi. Marcel was already elbow deep into his pineapple carving, so that was the one thing Ace didn't have to worry about.

Looking at the clock, Ace began to panic for the first time. He realized that he'd let his relationship with Ronnie interfere with his drive to win. Had he really just given up the best ingredients just so she wouldn't be angry with him? And for what? Her mood toward him still seemed to be as sour as ever.

Ace stared at his ingredients but nothing was coming together in his head. For the first time since he agreed to compete, he was worried that he might not make it any further.

Ronnie stood before the judges confidently. Despite her rocky start, she and LQ had remained focused and had worked together like a well-oiled machine. Instinctively, Ronnie knew she was about to present the best dish she'd made in a *Food Fight* challenge to date.

"Welcome, Ronnie," the host said as the camera panned over her presentation. "Would you please explain to the judges what you've prepared for them today?"

As soon as she'd had the taro, ahi and the huli-huli sauce laid out before her, a dish began to formulate in her mind.

"I seared the ahi and flavored it with a spicy fruit salsa and stacked it on a bed of crunchy taro chips. I like to call them huli-huli chips because they'll make you want to do the hula-hula," she said, swaying her hips in a hula dance.

The judges nodded, starting to sample her dish. Kari Voegler looked up and smiled. "Ronnie, after the mix-up with the ingredients, you had the opportunity to choose which protein and spice you wanted to keep. You made a risky choice by keeping the huli-huli sauce with the tuna instead of the pork. What made you decide to do that?"

"Huli-huli sauce is a marinade of ginger and soy sauce that's similar to teriyaki, so yes, it would have been a brilliant match with the pork. But my other option was wasabi, which I'd used in my first-round dishes. I chose the huli-huli sauce because I didn't want you all to accuse me of being a one-trick pony. Taking the ahi was a no-brainer. It was a beautiful cut, and I was excited to use it."

Chef Sam Lomi spoke next. "I love the huli-huli chips you made from the taro."

Taro, a purple root used in the traditional Hawaiian poi, was known to be gluey and bland. It would have been easy for Ronnie to panic when she saw it in her box. Instead of using the sauce on her fish, Ronnie chose to slice the taro thin, marinate it with huli-huli and deep-fry it into crispy chips.

"Taro is a tough ingredient to use," Chef Lomi continued, "and I'm impressed with your creativity as well as your flavors. Making the chips sweet instead of salty was an inspired choice. The contrast of the crunchy chips and the tender fish is delightful."

Ronnie breathed a sigh of relief. Her salt and sugar had been mislabeled, and the sweet instead of savory chips were a happy accident.

"I'd like to talk about your fruit carving," Chef Pelletier said.

Framing the fish platter were LQ's painstakingly carved tropical flowers made from mangos, melons, starfruit and pineapples.

"The carvings your sous chef created are bright and colorful. It's not overly complex, but they are beautiful and complement your plate."

Ronnie thanked the judges and headed back to the

canopied area where the other chefs were waiting. "This time, I'm not going to be at the bottom," she told herself.

Ace couldn't believe he was in the bottom two and now facing elimination. Once again, Etta Foster had come in first, and Ronnie, in a valiant comeback, had placed second with only two points keeping her from the top spot.

Sweat beaded on his brow as the host recapped the judges' comments. "Ace, the judges thought your spicy wasabi pulled pork and jicama salad were good but lacked creativity, but your tiki statue carved out of pineapples was impressive."

He shot Marcel a grateful look. If they made it out of this round, Marcel would get all the credit. They'd managed to dodge another disaster when they'd discovered that two of the feet on the base they'd brought for the sculpture had broken off. Thankfully, Marcel was able to think on his feet and prop up the base with carved fruit.

As for his part, Ace just hadn't been able to get his thoughts together fast enough to create a dish he could be proud of.

The host turned to Stewart's workstation. "Stewart, your ingredients were breadfruit, dried beef and soy sauce. The judges thought your presentation was beautiful but your flavors were overpowered by too many components.

"The question of the day is, Who will be going home, and who will move on to compete in Paris against Etta Foster and Veronica Howard?"

Ace held his breath as the announcer paused during what had to be the longest thirty seconds of his life. He'd never once imagined that he would mess up so completely. If he was sent home—

"Stewart Compton, you've been knocked out and will not move on in the *All-star Food Fight*."

Stewart let out a dramatic shriek. But all Ace could hear was his own breath pouring out of his lungs in one long, relieved sigh. He didn't ever want to feel this way again.

It was okay to lose. If he wasn't as good as his competitors, he was man enough to face that. But today he'd nearly defeated himself. He'd let his emotions stand in the way of doing his best, and he couldn't afford to let that happen again.

He looked across the yard at Ronnie, where she was standing with Etta Foster and their sous chefs. Ronnie still wouldn't look at Ace.

"That was a close one, buddy." Garett had jogged over to clap him on the back. "I have to admit, you had me sweating there for a minute."

Looking into his friend's eyes, a sinking sensation washed over Ace. Was it possible that Ronnie had overheard him speaking with Garett last night? They'd been talking in the hallway outside his room. If she'd decided to come after him—

He shook his head at Garett. "Oh man, Ronnie's not speaking to me, and I think it may be all your fault."

His friend blanched. "Me? What did I do? I haven't even spoken to her."

"I couldn't find her after we talked last night, and she's been giving me the cold shoulder all day. I think she might have overheard us in the hallway."

Garett shrugged. "So? What could we have said that was so bad?"

"Are you kidding me? I was telling you to call off the publicity stunts, and you were talking about showmances and me being free to date other women. Now she probably thinks our entire relationship was nothing but a publicity stunt cooked up by you."

Garett grimaced. "Yeah, that sounds like something I would do. Well, all you have to do is set her straight."

Ace chewed his lower lip. "It's going to be nearly impossible to convince her to see me at this point."

"Then cut your losses. To be honest, after your piss-poor performance today, it's clear that this relationship is nothing but a distraction. She's the enemy, for heaven's sake. If you want to get it on with her, you should wait until the competition is over."

"That's what I've been trying to tell him," Marcel chimed in as he cleared off their workstation.

Ace rubbed his temples. Things would be so much simpler if he just wrote the whole thing off. But he wasn't ready to do that. And the thought of letting her think he'd been playing her this entire time made him feel sick.

"I know what you both think, but I have to clear the air with her. Regardless of what goes on between us, from now on nothing is going to stand in the way of my winning this competition. I can promise you both that much."

Both men gave him skeptical grumbles, but Ace's mind had already moved on. How was he going to get Ronnie to listen to him, and more importantly, believe him?

He'd already spent half the previous evening and part of the morning calling her. If she wouldn't answer then, she wasn't going to answer now. And that made it a safe bet that she wouldn't open the door to him if he knocked.

Suddenly, an unconventional solution came to mind. Perhaps what he needed was a little hair of the dog that bit him.

Ace turned to Garett. "Do you think you can use your powers for good instead of evil?"

His friend shook his head. "Hmm, it's not really my area of expertise."

Grabbing Garett by the arm, he said, "It is now. I need your help."

Back in her room that evening, Ronnie tried not to think about Ace as she packed her bag. Tomorrow the remaining chefs in the competition would fly to the GTV studio in California to do the voice-overs for the first two rounds of the *All-Star Food Fight*.

The final round in Paris would tape live next week after a special double episode of the first two rounds aired that weekend.

Ronnie took the last three dresses out of her closet and placed them in her garment bag. She'd avoided packing them until now because they were the ones Ace had helped her pick out in Las Vegas. Now, staring at the empty closet, she'd been tempted to leave them hanging there. But they'd cost her too much money for that. But the bikini, which she hadn't paid for, was in the trash can.

The phone in her room rang and Ronnie didn't answer it. It was probably Ace again, and she had nothing to say to him. Seconds later, her cell phone rang. She saw Cara's picture and tapped the answer button.

"Hi, Cara."

"Ronnie," her friend said. "You've got to go online. There's something you've got to see."

Cara had always been a computer geek, but Ronnie had never gotten too involved with them herself. "Girl, you know I don't have a computer here. Why don't you just describe it to me? What is it—dancing babies or some talking animals on YouTube?"

"I can't describe it. You have to see it for yourself. And

trust me, you don't want to miss this. Just go look. Your phone has internet access."

Confused but curious, Ronnie sat down and let her friend talk her through the process of pulling up an internet video on her phone.

"Okay, now we have to hang up while you watch it," Cara instructed. "But call me when you're done."

Ronnie navigated to the link Cara had told her to and found herself watching streaming video on the Entertainment News channel. A reporter was holding a microphone out to Ace, and Ronnie caught her breath.

"This can't be good," she muttered.

"There's been a lot of buzz in the last few days about a budding romance between you and one of the chefs you're competing with on Gourmet TV's *All-Star Food Fight*. Are you finally ready to comment on this?"

"Yes, actually, I have a lot to say on this topic because the press and my overzealous publicist have joined together to get me in trouble with my lady. She seems to think our romance is just an elaborate publicity stunt. Right now, I want to tell her, and the world, that I'm in love with her. My feelings for her are real, and I'm hoping that she'll talk to me and give me a chance to explain things in person."

Unsure what to make of this spontaneous confession, all Ronnie could do was stare at the screen and blink. He loved her? Then why had he thought doing an online interview would be the appropriate way to tell her? Wasn't this just more promotion for his book?

Apparently, the reporter thought so. "You do have a new cookbook coming out soon, don't you?"

Ace shrugged. "Actually, I've said all I came to say. Thanks for your time." Then he walked off camera.

As Ronnie sat, shaking her head in disbelief, there was

a knock at the door. Still deep in her thoughts, she absently stood to open the door.

"Can we talk?" Ace said, from the hallway.

Ronnie frowned, looking back at the phone. "I thought you were online."

"I taped that in the hotel lobby two hours ago," he said, walking over to her.

Ace pushed her open suitcase aside and sat down on the edge of her bed. "Look. When you disappeared last night and wouldn't return my calls, I realized you must have overheard me talking to Garett in the hallway last night. Is that right?"

Ronnie nodded. "That's right. I heard him admit that you got involved with me just for the publicity."

"That conversation was out of context. From the beginning he could see that I was attracted to you. He started joking, I *thought,* that a showmance would be a great press angle. I kept telling him to forget about it, but Garett is headstrong, and because he's a friend, I guess I've always given him too much freedom when it comes to my career. Once we got together, he started leaking it to the press. I didn't even know what he was doing until it was too late."

Ronnie sighed. "And when was that? When you didn't say anything to me about it in Las Vegas? Or when you didn't say anything about it to me at the lagoon?"

"You're right," he said, running his hands over his bald head. "I should have told you what was going on when I figured out what Garett was up to. But I wanted to set him straight first. We started playing telephone tag and then I finally tracked him down last night. That's why I left you to go meet him. When I came back, I was going to tell you everything. Unfortunately, you were already gone."

Ronnie shrugged. "Whatever."

"Whatever?" He frowned at her. "Is that all you have to say?"

"Yeah. Whatever. There's nothing more for me to say."

"I meant what I said today, Ronnie. I love you. My feelings for you are real. They always have been."

Ronnie looked into his eyes, and she wanted to believe him. "You sound convincing, but the truth is, all along you've been trying to make me into something that I'm not. The real me was never good enough for you."

"What are you talking about?"

"You've been dressing me up like some doll, picking out sexy outfits and skimpy bikinis, so I'll be more like the girls you usually date. Maybe that's just not who I am. What about that?"

Ace threw up his hands. "That's crazy. I wasn't trying to make you over. Picking those clothes was an innocent gesture."

"Maybe it was, maybe it wasn't, but until this competition is over, I can't continue to worry about this."

He rolled his eyes. "This competition is really all you care about, isn't it. Is winning really the only thing that matters? I can't help wondering what you wouldn't do to win this thing."

Ronnie's spine snapped straight. "What are you implying?"

"Oh, nothing. Just that maybe all the mishaps in the kitchen ultimately worked to your advantage today."

"Are you accusing me of sabotage?" she scoffed. "That's funny, since you're the one who ended up with two proteins. You didn't even speak up about it until I complained. Maybe you were hoping to keep your advantage."

"That wasn't an advantage, and I *was* going to speak up when the judges got to my table."

"By then it may have been too late to make adjustments. Were you also the one who switched the salt and sugar in my station?"

"Listen, I don't need to stoop to petty tricks to beat you in this competition, Ronnie. I've proven that many times over. Maybe you're the one who broke the stand for our fruit carving. It wasn't damaged until today."

Ronnie was so angry all she could do was stare daggers in Ace's direction. "This conversation isn't getting us anywhere. But one thing is clear. We don't trust each other. And that's certainly not a foundation for any kind of relationship. I think you should leave now."

Ace stared at her in openmouthed silence as if waiting for something to change. Finally, when nothing did, he stood and walked out the door.

Chapter 15

Ace felt like a caged animal. In a few minutes, their plane from Kauai to California would be taking off, and he had nowhere to run. He was in a left aisle seat and Ronnie was across the aisle in the right window seat.

Of course he was seated near the last person he wanted to see. That's how his luck was going these days.

He refused to look in her direction. He didn't have to look to know she was going out of her way to ignore his existence. Their argument last night had been one of the worst he'd ever had with anyone. And after watching his parents bicker and take petty shots at each other when he was young, he'd made it a point to avoid that kind of bitter confrontation.

Picking up the in-flight magazine, Ace blindly flipped through the pages. Maybe this failed attempt at a real relationship was just confirmation that he wasn't cut out for one.

His grand gesture, confessing his love for her on the internet, had backfired. She'd rejected him outright. Ronnie was so focused on winning the *Food Fight* that she hadn't wanted to work things out.

Now, for his trouble, he had fallen into last place in the competition. Did he really believe that she'd tried to sabotage his kitchen? No. But it had been the only thing he could say to lash out at her. It hurt that she cared more about winning than she cared about him.

For all he knew, she really believed he was capable of the things she'd accused him of. But they'd been friends for years—she should know him better than that.

Friends. Now they didn't even have that between them. How had things gone so terribly wrong?

Ace closed his eyes, wishing this plane was headed home to New York.

Normally, Ronnie would have been completely preoccupied with the fact that Ace was sitting just a couple of feet away. But, as the plane began to taxi down the runway, she realized she had a much bigger problem to deal with.

Somewhere between Washington, D.C., and Hawaii, she'd developed a very real fear of flying. She'd never been comfortable with air travel, but now she was facing full-on panic.

The businessman in the seat next to her had taken the armrest, and while Ronnie wasn't normally rude, this was an emergency.

She moved her arm over until she could clutch the armrest as tight as possible. The man turned his head sharply to stare at her, but she ignored him. He should have been glad she hadn't grabbed his arm for support. In a crisis, personal boundaries were null and void.

She heard the roar of the engine and knew the plane

was about to take off. Ronnie could feel the sweat beading on her forehead, and she suddenly felt as though it was a struggle to breathe. Her chest constricted in pain as though someone were stabbing her. Anxiety attack, her mind told her. She'd had a roommate in college who'd had them all the time.

Not wanting to start screaming hysterically, she pressed her eyes closed and began repeating reassuring thoughts in her head.

Ronnie hadn't realized that she'd been mumbling "You're not going to die," out loud until she felt a hand cover hers on the armrest and a deep voice whispering, "It's going to be okay."

Startled, Ronnie looked up and found herself staring at Ace. Looking across the aisle she saw the businessman sitting in the seat Ace had vacated.

Ace squeezed her fingers, "I know you're afraid of flying. I'll help you through this…if you want me to."

Too scared for pride, Ronnie swallowed hard and nodded. The plane was still angled upward into the sky. This was always the worst part for her. It was like the painstakingly slow climb up the incline on a roller coaster. Once they leveled out, and the ride was underway, she'd be fine. At least she hoped so.

"Don't worry. Nothing's going to go wrong. And just think, even in the unlikely event that the plane did go down, the three of us are all here together," he said, nodding to the front row where Etta Foster and her grandson and sous chef, Adrian, were seated. "Nobody could win the *Food Fight*."

It shouldn't have made her laugh, but it did. Ace continued to talk to her, never letting go of her hand. Half the time, Ronnie didn't even know what he was saying. She just focused on his voice and the firm grip of his fingers.

A few moments later, the pilot told them they'd reached their cruising altitude, and Ronnie began to relax. Realizing that she was doing better, Ace let go of her hand.

Ronnie immediately missed his touch. It was an overwhelmingly kind gesture for him to come to her when she needed him. Especially after the horrible things they'd said to each other the night before.

"Ace, thank you for—"

"You don't have to thank me."

"No, really, I do. I was seconds away from having a complete breakdown."

"No problem. I wouldn't sit by and watch you suffer—no matter what kind of person you think I am." He tried to lighten his tone with a laugh, but it fell short of the mark.

Heat spread over Ronnie's face. Now she regretted some of the things she'd said. They'd been friends for many years. He'd deserved the benefit of the doubt.

"I'm sorry. Last night, I didn't mean to say—"

He held up his hand. "We both said things that we regret. I think the pressure of the competition has gotten the best of both of us."

Reaching up, she took his hand just as he'd done when she was having her panic attack. She squeezed his fingers gently until he finally turned to look at her.

"I hate the idea of us not being friends anymore. Is it too late to go back?"

"I don't know. It's hard not to think of you as more than a friend."

"I was scared," she whispered. "Too scared to believe you when you said you loved me. Too scared to trust you. But, most of all, too scared to trust myself. I'm starting to fall for you, too, but with my track record, that can only mean one thing. And that's to run as fast as I can in the opposite direction."

Ace's eyes softened. "I'm sorry if I was rushing you. I guess I felt I had to step things up because I felt you slipping away. Maybe cooling things off is best for both of us. I do still want to be your friend."

Ronnie sighed with relief. "I'm so glad to hear that. Maybe, after the competition—"

"You don't have to say any more. After I came in last in the second round, I had to promise Marcel and Garett that I'd keep my head in the game. No more getting distracted by my beautiful competition."

She smiled, then hesitated. There was still one more thing she needed to know before the air would be clear between them.

"At the risk of ruining things again, there's still something bothering me."

Ace sighed. "Go ahead. Get it off your chest."

After their difficult conversation, Ronnie found it even harder to get the words out. She hoped asking wouldn't make things worse. "LQ told me that you used to date one of her model friends from New York. She says that you used her fame to get free publicity for your restaurant, and then, after your opening, you dumped her. Is that true?"

Ace snorted. "You must be talking about Mariah. What actually happened was that GTV was hiring models as background for my show. She thought I had some influence in who they chose. When she found out that I didn't, she dumped me."

Ronnie frowned. "Then why would she tell LQ that you dumped her?"

Ace shrugged. "If I knew why women did anything, I'd be a rich man. You may not believe me, but *The Sexy Chef* was just getting ready to air when my second restaurant was opening. I really didn't need the reputation of a model to promote it."

She nodded. His explanation made perfect sense. Now she was sorry she'd even asked. But it was too late for her to take it back. And so much had gone on between them over the last two weeks.

Ronnie hoped that they'd be able to salvage some sort of friendship from the wreckage, but as Ace put headphones in his ears and closed his eyes, she couldn't help wondering if it was too late for that, too.

Chapter 16

After the studio taping in California, the chefs had a couple of days off before traveling to Paris for the final round in the *Food Fight* competition.

Ronnie had never been to Paris, so she planned to fly over early with Cara and do some sightseeing. But first she went home for two days to play with her dog, Baxter, check in on Crave and visit her family.

On her last day home, Ronnie drove to her mother's house in Maryland where she'd grown up. Her mother, Sadie, and her 87-year-old grandma, Patsy, lived there. Ronnie often worried about the two of them alone there together, but somehow they managed.

As soon as she let herself into the house she could smell fresh-baked cherry pie, her favorite, fried chicken and corn bread. Her stomach growled in excitement. Coming home was hands-down the toughest part of maintaining her diet.

Ronnie walked through the house toward the kitchen, calling, "Mom? Grandma? I'm home."

When she entered the kitchen she found the two little old ladies sitting at the table peeling potatoes. Her mother eyed her from across the table. "Veronica, it's about time you came home. Nowadays we have to turn on the TV if we want to see you."

Ronnie leaned over to kiss her grandma on the cheek and the woman grabbed her wrist. "Child, you're skin and bones. You can't let yourself waste away to nothing. Now sit down and eat."

The Howard women were traditionally full-figured, and ever since Ronnie had lost weight her mother and grandmother had never let her hear the end of it.

"Actually, Grandma, I think I gained five pounds while I was traveling. I have to be very strict with my diet while I'm here."

"Five pounds," her mother scoffed. "I've never heard such nonsense. The mashed potatoes aren't ready yet, but there's plenty of chicken and corn bread. Grab yourself a plate."

It was futile to argue, so Ronnie put a sliver of corn bread and one drumstick on her plate. Grandma Patsy pulled down her glasses to stare at Ronnie's portion. "We don't keep any birds in here, Veronica. Go back and get yourself a human-size portion."

Laughing, Ronnie shook her head. They went around and around like this every time. "Human-size? Look at all those potatoes you two are peeling. I hope you all are expecting more company because you've got enough to feed an army."

"Give up, Ma," Sadie told her mother. "Veronica's one of those modern women now that don't believe in eating.

At least we can be sure that we taught her to cook properly. Tell us about the competition, sweetie."

As Ronnie peeled the skin off her drumstick under the glaring eyes of the two women, she described the whirlwind of activity surrounding the first two rounds. She purposely left out the parts involving Ace, which made Ronnie realize just how much he'd become a part of her life. She studied her two mentors sitting across the table from her.

"Mom? Grandma? Do you two ever regret not remarrying after your husbands left?"

Sadie rolled her eyes. "Lord, no. I can do bad all by myself. I don't need the help of a man."

Grandma Patsy nodded. "That's right. They're all liars and cheaters."

Ronnie nodded, staring down at her hands. "I guess it is easier to be on your own. A strong woman doesn't need a man."

Both women stopped peeling potatoes to stare at her. "What?" Ronnie asked, looking back at them.

"We didn't mean for you, child," Grandma Patsy said. "You're too young to give up on men."

"That's right," her mother said, shaking her peeler at her. "I need grandbabies. I don't care what kind of modern woman you are, you'll need a man for that."

"Huh? But, the two of you have always said—"

"Oh, Veronica," her mother said with a sigh. "We talk a lot of mess, but that's just talk. Do you think I don't wish for a man every time the lawn needs mowing?"

"And somebody to warm your feet under the covers when it's cold outside," Grandma Patsy said.

Ronnie shook her head in shock. In all her years growing up in that house, she'd never once heard her mothers admit that they missed the companionship of a man.

Her mother looked her in the eye. "Listen, Veronica, just

because our marriages didn't work out doesn't mean that you won't find a good man one day. We may have forgotten to mention it, but the truth is, they do exist."

Grandma Patsy nodded.

"They're hard to find, though," Sadie continued. "So when you come across one, you'd better hold on to him."

"And ask if he has a single grandfather for me," Grandma Patsy said, laughing.

"Cara, I can't believe you're eating hamburgers in Paris. You should be eating something more French, like croissants or vichyssoise."

"Here, this is French," Cara said, shoving a French fry in her mouth.

They were sitting at a café close to the Eiffel Tower. Unfortunately, the trip wasn't the week-long girlfriend bonding time she'd expected. When Cara told her that she wanted to bring her husband and kids to Paris with her, Ronnie couldn't say no.

As it was, during the last three days they'd been in France, Cara had sent A.J. and her children off on their own as much as she could so that she and Ronnie could have girl time. But this was the most romantic city on earth, and Ronnie didn't want to keep her friend from experiencing it with her husband.

"Besides," Cara said, "you've forced me to have rich French food for three days straight. I practically have crème brûlée coming out of my ears. This morning the hotel even served it with breakfast."

"And you combat rich French food with a hamburger and fries?"

"It's comfort food. It reminds me of home." Cara paused, making a face at her. "Have we switched bodies? I'm usually hassling you about eating burgers and fries.

I'm impressed with how dedicated you've been to your diet. But when I get home I'm going to have to lose a few pounds."

Ronnie rolled her eyes. "Don't worry, fat doesn't dare stick to your skinny frame. You've scared it away permanently from your years of cardio."

Cara finished her hamburger and wiped her hands on her napkin. "How are you holding up? Are you still upset about Ace?"

Ronnie waved off her friend. "I'm fine. Like I told you, we cleared the air on the plane. We probably won't be as close as we once were, but we've agreed to be friends."

"That's a start."

Ronnie shook her head. "Or maybe it's a finish. I won't know until we see each other again. But what matters now is getting through this last leg of the *Food Fight*."

Even as she said the words she didn't quite believe them. Something felt very empty inside her since she'd broken things off with Ace. And ever since the startling revelation that her mothers didn't hate men as much as they pretended, Ronnie had been more confused than ever.

The truth was, these last few days in Paris had been lonely. Sure, Cara had made a point to spend a day at the spa with her getting massaged with chocolate-infused oils. They'd shopped on the Avenue des Champs-Élysées, and that morning they'd gone to the top of the Eiffel Tower.

But the rest of the time Ronnie had insisted that Cara do things with her family. They always invited Ronnie to tag along, but after eating dinner with them the first night, she realized that it was less painful to order room service in her hotel room.

Seeing the happy family looking picture perfect made her realize that she was over thirty and without a family of her own. In the past she'd spent a lot of time with Cara's family and that fact had never bothered her. But somehow things were different now.

In order to keep her friend from feeling sorry for her, she always claimed she was going to do something with LQ. There had been some tension between Ronnie and her sous chef at first, but after a long talk over lunch, things had lightened up between them. Still, when LQ asked her to spend time with her and her husband, she didn't always go. Right now, it was tough to be a third wheel.

Most of the time Ronnie was on her own—window shopping, sightseeing and sampling French cuisine. While she *was* lonely, she took the time to sort through her emotions. Her friends meant well, but she didn't want to have to pretend to be upbeat when she wasn't.

The competition was in three days, and she'd spent a lot of time thinking about what the judges might ask them to prepare. No one knew what the final *Food Fight* challenge would be, but Ronnie made sure she was prepared.

She studied French recipe books, visited restaurants and spoke with the chefs, keeping her mind focused on the things she knew she could do best.

When it was time to compete, Ronnie knew she'd be ready. But for the moment, she just wished she could have a little taste of the romance Paris seemed to demand.

Ace got off the elevator and entered the hotel lobby after spending most of the day sleeping. He was in Paris a few days early, but he wished he wasn't. Unfortunately, he'd taken a leap of faith and booked his plane tickets months in advance, not knowing he'd be so reluctant to tour the city.

It had been only three months since his last visit, and while he'd had a great time tasting the local flavors and meeting new people, he hadn't forgotten how lonely the place had made him feel.

He wasn't looking forward to dining alone in spots better suited to couples or strolling along the Seine by himself. Taking out his phone, he searched for Marcel's number. He knew he'd brought Simone along for the final leg of the competition, but at this point, being a third wheel would be better than being on his own.

As he scrolled through his contact list, he almost ran into someone headed toward the elevators. *"Excusez-moi,"* he muttered without looking up.

"My, aren't you fancy, with the French just rolling off your tongue."

Surprised at the familiar female voice, he looked up to see Ronnie standing before him. Immediately, his spirits lifted. "Ronnie, I'm sorry. I didn't see you there. Where are you headed?"

"Back to my room to order room service." She held up a shopping bag. "I was out buying souvenirs for my staff back home."

Ace felt like a teenager, with his heart hammering in his chest at the sight of her. "I'm headed out to find some place to eat. I—" He swallowed, almost changing his mind. "I don't suppose you'd like to join me?"

With the words out, he braced himself for her rejection.

"Uh, sure. Do you mind waiting while I dump this stuff in my room and freshen up a bit?"

She said yes! "No problem. I'll wait for you here," he said, almost feeling giddy.

To his relief, Ronnie was only gone only a few moments. Because during that time he'd managed to convince himself that she wasn't coming back. When had he become so vulnerable?

Coming toward him she looked great in her dark denim jeans, purple camisole and long black sweater. Her hair was pulled back from her face, but fell long around her shoulders. She looked soft and pretty.

He wanted to kiss her.

Blinking rapidly, he pushed those thoughts aside. Just because she'd agreed to have dinner with him didn't mean she would let him kiss her. She'd made it clear that all she wanted from him was friendship.

"So where are we going for dinner?" she asked when she reached his side.

"When I was here a few months ago, I found some great places we could try. What are you in the mood for?"

"Why don't you surprise me?"

They left the hotel, and Ace hailed a cab. He enjoyed the chance to show off his French. He instructed the driver to take them to a little bistro owned by a well-known French chef.

If Ace was afraid the dinner conversation would be awkward after all they'd been through recently, he was wrong. They'd fallen back into the rhythm of the lighthearted banter they'd shared in culinary school.

The food was amazing, the company was wonderful and Ace felt happier than he had in a while. The only thing hanging over him on the cab ride back to the hotel was that it would be over soon.

The sky was darkening and they were nearing the Eiffel Tower. "Have you been to the Eiffel Tower yet?"

She nodded. "Yeah, Cara and I went this morning."

"Have you seen it at night?"

"No," Ronnie said, laughing. "Is there much to see at night?"

"They light it up. Do you want to see?"

She shrugged. "Yeah, okay."

Ace told the cab driver where to go. There was a concrete viewing area between two buildings across the way from the Eiffel Tower. From there they had a perfect view of the tower twinkling at night with white sparkling lights.

"This is a great view," Ronnie said. "I never would have guessed that it would be worth seeing at night even more than during the day. Thanks for not letting me miss this."

"You're welcome," he said, standing a bit behind her. For a moment they just stood silently, staring at the twinkling tower. This was one of the romantic activities that he'd had to do alone the last time he was here.

He wanted to wrap his arms around her and rest his chin on the top of her head. But he also didn't want to ruin the moment by doing something she didn't want him to do. Still, the urge in him was strong. Inching forward, he moved up until her back was against his chest. She didn't move away.

Taking a deep breath, he slipped his arms around her waist. He felt her lean back on him, covering his hands with hers. Smiling, Ace tightened his arms around her, letting his chin drop onto her head.

They stood there watching the Eiffel Tower sparkle for several more minutes. Finally, he pulled back and Ronnie turned in his arms. Then, as if it were the most natural thing in the world, Ace leaned down and kissed her.

When the kiss broke, he said, "We can probably walk back to the hotel from here. Do you want to?"

She smiled up at him. "Let's do it."

As they entered their hotel lobby, Ronnie's heart began to race. She'd had a wonderful evening with Ace and she wasn't ready for it to end.

For the last couple of hours she hadn't had to think

about the competition or relationships. And best of all, she'd finally been able to appreciate the inherently romantic atmosphere that Paris had to offer.

They walked back to their hotel, holding hands while Ace tried to teach her key phrases in French. Soon they were back at the hotel and the only thing left to do was say good-bye.

Ace hit the up button on the elevator and they stepped inside.

"Do you want to come up to my room for a little while?" Ronnie asked. "The hotel gave me a complimentary bottle of champagne."

A wide smile broke out on Ace's face. "Yes, I'd like that."

Ronnie let Ace into her room, knowing in the back of her mind that she was treading on dangerous territory. But she ignored that nagging feeling because being with Ace felt so good at the moment. And after so many days of feeling bad, she wasn't ready to give that up.

If she stopped to examine the situation, she'd be forced to admit that this was her old pattern. She chose what felt good over what was good for her. That's how she'd woken up and found herself overweight one day.

But that was a problem for another time.

Ronnie opened her minibar and pulled out the champagne. She turned to find Ace standing over her. He took the bottle out of her hand and placed it on top of the bar.

"I missed you," he said simply, and Ronnie felt herself break.

"I missed you, too," she said. Then their mouths came together urgently.

Chapter 17

Ace slid his hand behind Ronnie's neck, tilting her face so he could deepen their kiss. His other arm locked around her waist, holding her tight and close.

He slipped his tongue between her lips. He'd missed the heat of her mouth. His hands slid down her body. He'd missed her soft, supple curves. She moaned his name.

Afraid a false move or stray word would shatter this fragile moment, Ace pulled Ronnie over to the bed and began undressing her. But as her fingers burrowed under his T-shirt to help him pull it off over his head, he saw no sign of second thoughts in her eyes.

Ace didn't waste time questioning this unexpected good fortune. He lay back on the bed and lifted Ronnie over him. He wanted her to take the lead.

Relishing the opportunity, she surprised him by leaning over until her lips grazed his chest. Then they made a whisper-soft trail over the planes of his stomach. His abdomen contracted as her tongue circled his navel and continued downward.

When she reached the apex of his thighs, she cupped him in her hands and lowered her mouth over him. Ace squirmed against the sheets as she licked from the base to the tip like an ice cream cone on a summer day.

Ronnie worked him with her lips and tongue until Ace thought he'd go out of his head. Hoping to take back control, he dragged her up his body, groaning at the torturous friction.

Rolling her beneath him, he began his own assault on her senses. First he used his teeth to lightly nip at her breasts, then soothed his bites with the suction of his mouth. Before long she was writhing against the bed just as he'd done moments earlier. But Ace wasn't done with his sensual torment.

Taking the same journey down Ronnie's body that she'd taken over his, he found her sensitive folds. Lovingly, he kissed and licked her until she was nearly screaming his name. Despite her protests, he didn't quit until he felt her body quiver with pleasure.

Then, knowing he'd held on as long as his body could, he put on protection and buried himself inside her. Their bodies rocked together in several long strokes, and Ace knew he was about to fall over the edge.

Thankfully, Ronnie began to tremble, freeing him to enjoy his own release. Exhausted, they fell asleep in each other's arms.

Ronnie awoke in the middle of the night disoriented. She shivered, not sure if it was a bad dream or something else that had caused her to sit straight up in bed.

Then it was as if all her demons and insecurities came to haunt her at once—worries over the competition, pressure to stay thin while surrounded by some of the most decadent food in the world, questions about whether it had been a mistake to be with Ace again.

Ronnie shifted to climb out of bed and a pair of steel arms slipped around her. Ace pulled her close, letting her rest her back against his chest as he held her.

"What's wrong? Did you have a bad dream?"

Ronnie felt like a fool. She couldn't find the words to express the fears that plagued her, so she shook her head.

"It wasn't a dream? Are you just overwhelmed?"

Sighing, Ronnie nodded.

He squeezed her tighter. "I know the feeling, but you can't let this competition get to you. It's just food. In the grand scheme of life, how much is this really going to matter down the road?"

She leaned back against his chest. "Probably not much."

"That's right. And I'm sure your mom and your grandma Patsy are proud of what you've achieved so far."

"Yeah, I think they are."

"Then take a deep breath and relax. You're an amazing, funny, beautiful woman and a talented chef. That's all you need to remember."

Ronnie sighed again. "Thanks, Ace. You always were good with words."

He laughed, squeezing her again. "Good with words, good with food, good with the ladies. You need to recognize… you're in the presence of greatness right now."

His words were so cocky and out of the blue, Ronnie found herself laughing out loud.

"That's more like it," he continued. "Stop and think about where you are right now. You're in Paris, France. About to cook in a television competition with two other world-class chefs. You're one of the best. How many people get opportunities like we have right now?"

"I know you're right. And I've tried to take it all in. I've toured the city, I ate in some of the most amazing restaurants, I talked with the chefs…. But there must be something wrong with me, because it left me kind of cold."

Actually the first time she'd begun to feel like she was truly enjoying herself was tonight. Having a simple meal with a man she liked, visiting the Eiffel Tower and strolling home made her finally feel a part of the romance of Paris.

"I know exactly what you're talking about. The last time I was here researching my cookbook, I was on my own. Suddenly everything seemed made for couples. It's much easier to appreciate this beautiful city when you have someone to share it with."

Ronnie nodded, feeling her heart rate picking up. She didn't want to think about how much she was letting herself lean on Ace. She didn't want to acknowledge the feelings that were chipping away at the walls around her heart.

"I have an idea," he said suddenly.

"Yes?"

"Why don't I show you Paris tomorrow. Now, before you tell me that you've already seen it, let me show you Paris my way. Some of the funky little places you may not have seen yet. We can do some of the things that I couldn't do on my own last time I was here."

Ronnie felt warm and safe in Ace's arms. And for now, she didn't want it to end. She'd just have to face the consequences later.

"That sounds like fun," she whispered. Then they both laid back and eventually drifted off to sleep, wrapped in each other's arms.

* * *

Ace woke up early the next morning, realizing that he'd have to work fast if he wanted to make good on his promises to Ronnie. He carefully climbed out of bed, trying not to disturb her in her sleep. As he pulled his pants back on, he couldn't help but watch as she lay peacefully on the bed.

She always came off confident and strong, and seeing her so upset made him want to cheer her up. He wanted today to be special. Their relationship was at a tenuous point. They'd agreed to keep things casual, and it hadn't taken long for them to push that aside.

Ace was well aware of the fact that she could back away from him again, if he gave her the chance.

He scrawled a note on the hotel pad, left it on his pillow and crept out of her room. He had several ideas for making it a fun day, but he was going to need some help from the hotel concierge to make everything come together.

Two hours later, after showering and changing into navy walking shorts and a gray polo shirt, he met Ronnie in the hotel lobby. The concierge had been very helpful, and Ace was excited to show Ronnie his first surprise.

She walked over to him and splayed her arms. "Am I dressed appropriately?"

Ace thought she looked cute in her khaki shorts, black tank and matching sweater. "Yeah, you look great. Are those shoes comfortable?" he asked, eyeing her black leather sandals.

"Yes, they have padded soles. Why, what are we doing?"

"You'll see as soon as we get outside."

Taking her hand, he led Ronnie through the hotel entrance. A red Vespa was parked at the curb. "This is our transportation for the morning."

Ronnie clapped her hands in delight. "This is great. I've always wanted to ride one of these. But is it safe?"

"I drove one all over the city last time I was here. There's a bit of a learning curve, but I'm an old pro with it now. I promise to take care of you."

"Okay, let's do it," Ronnie said, putting on the helmet he offered her.

She got on behind him and they took off. Ace gave her a brief tour of the city through his eyes, stopping frequently to share bits of trivia he'd picked up. Ronnie added in her own anecdotes, and they had a wonderful time.

After an amazing morning, Ronnie was stunned when Ace took her to a private room in the wine cellar of a French château for a wine-and-cheese tasting lunch.

"This is the most beautiful place I've ever visited," she said to Ace as their sommelier, Phillipe, poured them a glass of white wine and served them some rich, sharp cheeses with a baguette.

"I'm glad you like it. I have to admit, I'm pretty pleased I was able to pull this off on such short notice."

The sommelier poured five different wines for them over the course of the lunch, serving different meats, cheeses, fruits and breads that paired well with them.

After he was done with his presentation, Phillipe left them alone to help themselves to what remained.

"Uh-oh," Ronnie said, giggling.

Ace wiped his lips with his napkin. "What's wrong?"

"I think I may have drank too much. I'm feeling a little tipsy."

"That's okay. We don't have to leave right away. And I'm having a car pick us up, so you don't have to worry about getting back on the Vespa."

She shook her head. "That's not my problem."

He frowned. "What is it?"

"I don't usually drink much because wine…um, puts me in the mood."

"In the mood for—oh, I get it now. If I'd known that's all I had to do, we could have just stayed in the hotel room with a bottle of wine."

"How long will it take us to get back there?" she asked, circling the rim of her glass with her finger.

"Too long," he said. "We don't have to go back right away. We've got this room all to ourselves. No one will interrupt us."

"Are you sure? What about Phillipe?"

"He's not coming back. Come here."

Ronnie got out of her seat and walked over to straddle Ace. "Phillipe forgot to tell you what goes best with Château Margaux," she whispered.

"Oh, yeah? What?" he asked, slipping his hands around her waist.

Wrapping her arms around his neck, she sucked on his earlobe, then whispered softly, "Me."

Ronnie bent over to pick up her sweater from the cellar floor, then stood.

Ace gave her a sexy smile. "Are you ready to go?"

Even though she was no longer tipsy, Ronnie still felt giddy. "Yes," she said, giggling.

Taking her hand, Ace led her over to the heavy oak door of the cellar. It took two hands to pull it open.

They stepped through the opening and saw a tour group standing in the corridor admiring a long hall of tapestries while the guide described them.

Shocked, the two of them just stood there for a second. Ronnie, remembering her loud moans, felt an embarrassed heat rushing up her neck. Some of the tourists, having spotted them, were starting to snicker. Both of them realized at once that they had been overheard.

Ace grabbed her arm and they began weaving their way around the tourists until they could reach the stairs and make their exit.

Safely in the car, they headed back to their hotel, Ronnie buried her head in Ace's broad shoulder. "I still can't believe we just did that. When I saw all of those people standing out there, I thought I was going to die of embarrassment."

Ace laughed. "Who cares if they could hear us. We'll never see those people again. Besides, now you can't claim that you're not sexually adventurous. I think we've added a couple of daring escapades to your list."

"That's true."

Her time in Paris with Ace would make for some of the best memories of her life. Too bad they had to get back to reality when the competition started up again the next day. It had been wonderful to live in the fantasy for the last day and a half.

And after the competition was over… Well, she didn't even want to think about that. She and Ace didn't even live in the same state. There were so many reasons why they couldn't make this a long-term thing.

"You've grown quiet on me. What's wrong?"

"Nothing. I was just thinking about how much I enjoyed this day together."

"The day's not over yet."

"You can't possibly top what we did this afternoon," she said, resisting the urge to giggle again.

"Why don't you let me try?"

They walked into the lobby of their hotel hand in

hand, but as soon as the desk clerk saw them, she waved them over.

"We've been trying to reach you two. Your cooking competition is starting early. It will begin in two hours. You must dress and meet in the ballroom at six o'clock," she said, handing them envelopes from the Gourmet TV Network.

Ronnie and Ace exchanged harried looks. "We'd better go track down our sous chefs," Ace said.

"See you in the ballroom."

Without time to process the change in plans, they both got on the elevator and went their separate ways.

Back in her room, Ronnie called LQ's cell phone. LQ picked up with a panicked tone. "There you are. Did you get the message from Gourmet TV?"

"Yes, that's why I'm calling. Do you know what's going on?"

"Only that we're all meeting at six to find out. Where have you been? I've been calling your cell phone for the last hour."

"I was sightseeing. I must have had my ringer off."

"Okay, I guess it doesn't matter now. You got back in time. I'll see you there."

Ronnie hung up. It was just beginning to sink in how close she'd come to missing the start of the final leg of the *All-Star Food Fight*. Of course, Ace would have missed it, too.

What were they thinking giving them notice at the last minute? They wouldn't have been able to move forward without two of their contestants, would they? It wouldn't have been good television to let Etta Foster win by default.

Even though Etta was in the lead, Ronnie had to believe that she still had a shot at winning. There was still a chance that Etta could have an off day. Of course, the kitchen mishaps never seemed to rock Etta the way they had messed up her and Ace.

Swallowing hard, a terrible feeling washed over Ronnie. What if it wasn't a coincidence? Why were all the chefs plagued by mishaps with the exception of Etta Foster?

As the thought popped into her mind, she tried to push it out. It was hard to picture the grandmotherly figure doing anything sneaky or unethical. Of course, just because it was hard to believe didn't make it impossible.

Taking out the information packet sent by Gourmet TV, Ronnie found the producer's number on the bottom and dialed it.

"Ed Sims speaking," the producer answered.

"Hi, Ed, this is Ronnie."

"Hi, Ronnie, what can I do for you?"

"I have a question about the competition."

"I can't tell you what the next challenge is until to-night."

"My question isn't about tonight, it's about the previous rounds. Was GTV purposely messing up our equipment and ingredients to make the show more interesting?"

"No, those were just the realities of a live television show. It might not be a bad idea for future *Food Fights,* though. It's been a lot of fun watching you guys cook yourselves out of a corner."

"So you're saying that the missing or broken things that every chef has had are just coincidences."

"Yeah, of course. What else would it be?"

"Sabotage."

The man laughed. "Yeah, I guess it wouldn't be the first time."

"What? Are you serious?"

"I'm not saying anything for sure. I'm just saying it's

not the first time someone has blamed a problem in the kitchen on sabotage. Before the *Food Fights* we used to do an annual pie bake-off. One year the lead contender's stove went haywire and she never stopped claiming that she'd been sabotaged."

Ronnie's heart began to pound in her chest. "I used to watch that show. Wasn't that the year Etta Foster won for the first time? Her career really took off after that win."

Ed laughed. "Hey, you're right. I'd forgotten that she'd participated."

"Don't you think it's a bit of a coincidence that she's in the lead now after all the rest of us have been complaining of so many things going wrong? She hasn't seemed to have any problems at all."

Ed sighed. "I understand what you're saying, but there isn't much I can do about it. We don't have any proof. And just between you and me, I suggest you don't even bring this up again. Etta Foster is beloved by everyone at the network. If you start making accusations against her, it's just going to look like sour grapes. They'll think you're picking on a sweet old lady."

"You won't even investigate the possibility?"

"Investigate? How? Etta doesn't know what's coming up tonight just like the rest of you. Even if you believe she's been doing something to your kitchens in the past, there's no way she can sabotage you this time. I suggest you put your energy toward doing your best in this leg, and let your food speak for itself."

Ronnie hung up the phone steaming mad. The more she thought about it, the more she was convinced that Etta was behind these kitchen mix-ups. The chefs may not know what was ahead now, but that didn't mean Etta wouldn't find some way to mess them up before the entire thing was over.

Ronnie wasn't afraid to match her skills with Etta Foster or Ace. But she did want to make sure she started with a level playing field.

Picking up the phone she dialed Ace's number. "Can you and Marcel meet me in my room in ten minutes? I think we have a problem."

Chapter 18

Ace, Marcel and LQ all compared notes in Ronnie's room. It was clear now that Etta Foster wasn't the sweet grandmotherly type everyone believed her to be.

The question now was, how did they prove it?

"Now that I've talked to Ed on the phone, it's pretty obvious that, even if they suspect Etta themselves, they're not inclined to do anything about it without a lot of proof. They can't bring themselves to accuse a sweet little old lady of such crimes."

Ace nodded, deep in thought. "Then we're going to have to get our own proof."

LQ frowned at him. "How? There's no time. Apparently the competition is going to start in just over an hour."

Marcel nodded. "We don't even know what the competition is. Maybe it will be something she can't cheat at."

Ace shrugged. "There's got to be something we can do. We may have to wait until the competition is officially underway, but I don't think she's done messing us up."

Ronnie looked at the other chefs in the room. "We're just going to have to play it by ear. She can't make her move until she hears what the challenge is. And when she does try something, we're going to be ready for her."

The four of them tossed some ideas around and then went their separate ways to get ready.

Ronnie, LQ and the other chefs entered the ballroom to find out the next challenge. Everything was set up, but there was no live audience. The chefs had been told the live audience taping would be tomorrow.

The three chefs and their sous chefs were sent to their kitchens, and the cameras started rolling.

"We're here the day before our final *All-Star Food Fight* with our top three chefs for a special pre-round challenge. Right now, our chefs are going to find out for the first time exactly what their final challenge is. Are you all ready?"

The lights flashed in the studio, and Ronnie's heartbeat sped up. She crossed her fingers that it would be a challenge she could handle.

"The final round is a cake inspired by a landmark in Paris. We have cars parked outside our studio to take our chefs to any landmark they wish to use. If two chefs pick the same landmark, the first one to arrive there gets to use it. Once at the landmark, the chefs will be asked to sketch their cake design. Then they'll be brought back to the studio tonight to start baking the cakes they'll use to build their design in the studio tomorrow."

As soon as the host finished describing the challenge, Ronnie knew which landmark she wanted. The Eiffel Tower. She was afraid it might be a popular choice, so as soon as she, LQ and the cameraman climbed into their car, she instructed the driver to go.

As they were driving, Ronnie was asked to talk to the

camera about her choice and the reason behind it. She kept seeing an image in her mind of the Eiffel Tower sparkling with lights at night, and Ace kissing her in front of it.

She couldn't say any of that to the camera, so instead she said, "I think I'm going to make a wedding cake. Before I opened my restaurant, Crave, I used to make wedding cakes for the hotel where I worked. The Eiffel Tower may seem like an obvious choice, but I'm choosing it because it's Paris's most romantic icon. That's why it would be the perfect symbol of the vow between two people to spend the rest of their lives together."

Etta Foster had climbed into her car behind Ronnie, and glancing out the window, Ronnie realized Etta's car was following hers, turn for turn. As the Eiffel Tower came into view, Etta's car began to pass them.

"Vite, vite, s'il vous plait." She told the driver to go faster, using the limited French she'd learned from Ace.

The driver nodded and their car surged forward, edging in front of Etta's as they crossed through traffic trying to get close to the tower. As Ronnie's car pulled over, Etta's car sped away.

Ronnie looked back to LQ as she climbed out of the car. "I guess she knew it was pointless to get into a footrace with me."

Back at the set, Ace had just started pouring his cake batter into rectangular pans as the cameras came over to his kitchen. He'd had no competition traveling to the Arc de Triomphe, the large arch in the middle of Paris.

"My cake is going to be more of an architectural structure rather than just a cake. I'm going to bake oversized bricks that I can use to build the arch. I'm not a pastry chef, so I am a bit out of my element, but I think this is something I can do."

Ace tried to sound confident, but there was a lot to be done and he needed everything to go well if he was going to bring his vision to life. That meant he couldn't afford any inconvenient mishaps in this round.

Since they were baking the cakes tonight, he had a strong feeling that if anything were going to be sabotaged, it would occur overnight. They were going to have to find a way to make sure their cakes stayed untouched.

But there wasn't much time to strategize about that when he and Marcel had so much baking to do. They also mixed up a huge batch of icing to use on the crumb coating that would go beneath the fondant.

The Arc de Triomphe was a simple structure compared to Ronnie's Eiffel Tower and Etta Foster's Cathédrale Notre Dame, but Ace felt it was something he could do cleanly in the allotted time. If he was able to execute the cake well, maybe he could win this.

It was nearing midnight when all the chefs had finished baking their cakes and finally left the ballroom. Ronnie waited for Ace near the elevators and stepped inside with him.

"So, do you have a plan?"

Ace nodded. "Yes, I do. I had Marcel text Garett while we were baking. In a little while he's going to place video cameras in each of our kitchens so we'll be able to see if the cakes we baked are contaminated."

"When he recovers the cameras tomorrow, won't that be too late?"

"No, he'll be able to monitor the cameras on a live feed from his laptop. That way we don't have to lose sleep before the final leg of the competition. He'll call if he sees something shady."

Ronnie realized that with the rest of this sting operation

in Ace's hands, she was going to have to trust both him and Garett. It was an uncomfortable feeling, but she didn't have a lot of choices anymore.

"Okay, call me if anything turns up," she told him as Ace got off on his floor.

Around two thirty in the morning, Ronnie's telephone rang. Startled into full wakefulness, she grabbed the phone. "Yes?"

"We have some action in the kitchens," Ace said. "Someone came in and started tampering with your cakes and my royal icing. Etta's products weren't touched."

"Who was it?"

"We're not sure."

"I'll be right there." She started to climb out of bed.

"You don't have to come down now."

"But my cakes. I have to bake new ones."

"No, you don't. Garett is taking care of everything right now."

Ronnie blinked, still sleepy. "He's going to bake more cake for me?"

"No. It seems you and Etta are both doing round layer cakes. Her cakes are the same as yours. So he's switching your tampered cakes with her fresh ones and doing the same with her royal icing and mine."

Ronnie frowned. "Is that the right thing to do? Maybe we should just report the whole thing and let the judges decide how to handle it."

"We can do that. But I'm in favor of giving Etta Foster a little taste of her own medicine. When she walks into her kitchen tomorrow, she'll find the contaminated products she tried to make us use. Let's see if she's the star chef she thinks she is."

"I don't know."

"Look. You and I were able to make it through this competition despite working against the odds. If she's going to beat us fair and square, that's fine, but if she really deserves to win, she can triumph over the same odds we did."

"You've got a point there. But are you sure Garett can handle all of this by himself?"

Ronnie didn't like where her mind was going, but the thoughts came anyway. What if Garett only fixed Ace's problem and left her at a disadvantage with Etta. Then Garett's client, and his only real concern, Ace, would be a sure thing for the win.

"I know you must be worried, Ronnie. But I promise, neither he or I would screw you over just to win. I've never worked that way, and despite his obvious flaws, Garett doesn't either. I'll make sure of it."

"Okay," Ronnie replied, still not completely comfortable with the fact that everything was in Garett's hands now.

"Besides, if everything isn't just how it should be in your kitchen tomorrow, you can cry foul, and I'll back you up," Ace added. "We'll take our chances with the judges and let them sort it out. But I hope you can trust me."

"It's easier for me to trust you than it is for me to trust Garett."

"I know we don't have the best track record, but I wouldn't want to win if I had to do so at your expense. We've always had a *friendly* rivalry between us. I wouldn't stoop to dirty tricks now. I'm not afraid to lose to you, Ronnie. If you make the best cake tomorrow, I'll congratulate you. The fact that I plan to win doesn't take away from that fact."

Ronnie smiled. Ace hadn't ever shied away from a challenge in his life. Win or lose, he always fought hard.

And even though he could talk a lot of trash, he'd never been a sore loser.

She was going to have to trust him, because not doing so could cost her sleep, and she needed to put her best foot forward in the morning.

"I believe you, Ace. See you in the morning. You're going to need a good night's rest to handle the butt-whooping I'm going to hand you tomorrow."

The morning of the competition was a blur of activity for Ronnie. The first thing she and LQ did was inspect their prebaked cakes. They were light, fluffy and perfect. If Ronnie hadn't known better, she would have thought they were the cakes she'd baked herself.

There was some commotion in Etta's kitchen initially. She'd never seen a white-haired woman swear up such a blue streak.

"They've been switched. Someone switched my cakes. Look at them. They're falling apart."

Ronnie and LQ continued to work, and when the cameras arrived at her kitchen for her reaction to the accusations Etta was making, she played innocent.

"It seems Etta didn't bake a dense enough cake and now they're falling apart. I wish her luck. It's going to eat up a lot of her time if she has to start baking new cakes."

As the day went on, Ronnie heard that the judges had allowed Etta's sous chef, her grandson Adrian, to purchase new cakes at the market for her to use in the competition.

Beyond that, Ronnie didn't have time to worry about what was going on in the other kitchens. She wanted her Eiffel Tower wedding cake to be a showstopper.

At that moment, LQ was busy hand-pouring chocolate into the lattice shape of the top spire of the tower. Once the four sides of the candy pieces dried in the cooler, they would be constructed on top of the cake as the topper.

Ronnie planned to paint the rest of the towers by hand on the four round tiers below. The hand-painting would be the most time consuming portion of the cake, but if she could do clean work, she knew the judges would appreciate the detail. Especially Kari Voegler, who was a stickler for craftsmanship.

Now that all of her cake tiers were covered in smooth white fondant, she had a perfect blank canvas to showcase her artistry. Ronnie thought she had a genuine advantage in this leg of the competition, and she was excited to finally show what she could do under fair circumstances.

Ace had finished constructing and carving the shape of his arch for the Arc de Triomphe, and now that he'd covered it in fondant it was time to start carving the sculptures that were all around the archway.

If Ace had had more time, he would have special-ordered molds to fill with white chocolate to give a more authentic feel to his cake. Unfortunately, he didn't have that opportunity, so he was going to have to get creative.

He didn't have dainty little fingers to make the sculptures freehand out of chocolate, so he had to use modeling chocolate to form the general shape of the relief sculpture and then paint on the details. The result was that some of the elements would appear flat instead of raised. But it was the best he could do in the time he had left.

When the judges and the cameraman came around to his station, he had some tough questions to answer.

Kari Voegler, one of the *Food Fight*'s toughest judges, asked him, "In the other kitchens we have the Cathédrale Notre Dame and the Eiffel Tower. Do you think you've chosen a landmark that's complex enough?"

Ace smiled at Kari, but continued to work. "I'm not a pastry chef, so I chose something I thought I could do cleanly and completely in the allotted time. Hopefully, when you see my finished product, you'll like what I've done."

It didn't hurt to hope someone else in the competition messed up. There had been many cake challenges for the *Food Fight* where contestants didn't complete their cakes, or only vaguely represented the sketch they'd started with.

Ace and Marcel were working hard, so Ace had to hope *that,* along with the scores from his previous rounds, would be enough to put him over the edge.

From the quick look he'd given Ronnie's kitchen on his right, he could see that she was bringing her A game. He'd heard the interview she'd given about her chocolate spire at the top of the Eiffel Tower. With the delicate hand-painting she was doing on the cake, she was definitely the one to beat.

He didn't want to underestimate Etta Foster, but from the looks of her cake, she was grossly behind schedule. She had shed her grandmotherly image and was barking snide orders to her grandson. There were so many curse words flying out of her mouth, the producers had to warn her more than once.

She'd constantly complained about her cakes and her royal icing, and at this late stage in the competition, her cake barely resembled the Cathédrale Notre Dame.

But considering the fact that she'd won the first two rounds of the competition, it was possible that she'd take the top prize simply for completing her cake.

If that happened, he was worried that Ronnie may regret her decision to go along with his plan to let Etta drink her own medicine instead of trying to get her disqualified for cheating. But it was too late to turn back now.

There were only two hours left before they'd have their answer. Ace and Marcel just had to keep working.

Ronnie heard the audience counting down the clock just as she and LQ were trying to attach the chocolate spire to her Eiffel Tower cake. If they dropped it now, there was no time to make repairs.

The last leg of the spire was glued to the cake with royal icing and Ronnie instructed LQ to let go. They both stood back from the cake just as the buzzer sounded.

With a lump of pride in her throat, Ronnie surveyed her work. She'd carved the legs of the tower out of her round cake tiers, so that with all the layers stacked together, the Eiffel Tower appeared to be standing out from a round wedding cake. She'd meticulously piped the latticework of the tower's rails in chocolate so that it blended with the chocolate spire at the top. She'd decorated the rest of the wedding cake with traditional white icing decorations so that the tower was the main focus of the cake.

She'd never been more pleased with her work. She and LQ gave each other a high five. Now if she and LQ could just move the cake from their kitchen to the display table, Ronnie would be able to rest easy with the outcome of this competition, whatever it turned out to be.

It was a safe bet that Etta Foster wouldn't win this round. Her unfinished cake was being moved to the table as Ronnie awaited her own turn. Only half the elements in Etta's cake had made it onto her finished product. There were gaps and drooping frosting on the cake.

Ronnie watched as Etta and her grandson began to move their cake to the table. Etta was wearing a scowl that had been on her face since the start of this round. She was still muttering under her breath as they approached the table.

Adrian lifted his edge of the cake to move it over to the display table, but Etta seemed to give up at that point. A corner slipped out of her hand, and the cake dropped to the floor.

There was a startled gasp in the audience, and the announcer continued. "Etta Foster's entry is now just a pile of frosting on the floor. It's hard not to wonder if the perfectionist in Etta just wouldn't allow her to show an unfinished cake. Now we move to Ace Brown's kitchen where he'll be moving his Arc de Triomphe cake to the table."

With two strong men in that kitchen, no one was surprised when Ace and Marcel easily moved their showpiece to the table.

Now the final round would definitely go to either Ace or Ronnie. All she had to do was move her cake without incident, and she'd be in the running to win one hundred thousand dollars.

She and LQ each took two corners of the cake board and began to slide it off the counter. As soon as they began moving, her spire began to sway.

As if their minds were connected telepathically, both she and LQ froze. "Slowly, LQ. Very slowly. Let's move."

It was a delicate balancing act, but they took baby step after baby step toward the cake table. After what seemed like an eternity, Ronnie and LQ gingerly placed their cake on the table.

When the board was in place, Ronnie clutched her chest in relief and the audience exploded with applause.

Ronnie was riding a wave of elation as she and LQ entered the green room. It had been a long day, and after three very tough rounds, this competition was finally about to be over.

The last to place her cake, Ronnie was also the last to enter the green room. As she came in, she was surprised to find Etta Foster yelling at Ace.

Ace was sitting calmly as Etta ranted from across the room about her cake and icing being switched.

Ronnie glared at the woman. "Etta, you may as well admit that you cheated. Everyone in this room knows that you did. There are no cameras in here. Just admit it."

Etta glared back at her in surprise.

"It's true," Ace added. "Besides, how could you be so certain that your cake and icing had been switched, if you weren't expecting our kitchens to have the contaminated products? We saw Adrian on camera, Etta. If you don't want to admit the truth here in private, maybe you'd like to explain to the judges why Adrian was in our kitchens messing with our supplies last night."

Etta waved him off. "All right, all right. Why do you need me to say it out loud? You already know the truth."

Ronnie shook her head, confused. "I'd just like to know why a woman with your reputation in this industry would have to stoop to such low tactics. You're world famous and practically the face of GTV. Why didn't you go up against us fairly?"

She snorted. "The face of GTV? Maybe I used to be. But when it was time to renew my show's contract last month, the network told me they were going in a new direction. They want to pull in a younger demographic. Apparently I'm no longer relevant."

Ace tsked. "I'm sorry to hear that, Etta. But how does cheating to win help you stay relevant?"

"I can't afford to lose when they've already cancelled my show. I have to show that I *can* compete with you hotshot young chefs. I was planning to leverage this win into a pitch for a new show where I travel the country challenging young chefs to a cook-off."

Ronnie frowned. "Etta, if you feel you had to cheat in this competition, how were you planning to manage in your future challenges? Were you going to try to cheat your way through those, too? You're a talented chef. I'm sure you could have won without the underhanded tactics."

The older woman scowled. "We'll never know now. I guess it's time for me to retire anyway. All this travel has made me realize that I'd rather be at home."

Before they could discuss the matter further, the chefs were being called back out for the announcement of the winner.

Giving LQ a big hug, Ronnie left her with the other sous chefs backstage and lined up next to Ace and Etta for the announcement.

The host began to recap their scores from the previous rounds, and discussed the judges' comments on their cake presentations that day. Ronnie had received the highest praise of the day, but her scores going into this round were slightly below Ace's. With Etta receiving no points for this round, it was mathematically impossible for her to win.

Swallowing hard, Ronnie's mouth went dry as she waited for the verdict.

"The winner of Gourmet TV's *All-Star Food Fight…*" The announcer paused for effect.

Ace took Ronnie's hand and squeezed. They exchanged tense looks, but still managed to share a smile.

"With a final-round score just five points above the other chef, the winner of one hundred thousand dollars is Veronica Howard."

Chapter 19

Her win didn't start to sink in until LQ came out and a gold medal was placed over Ronnie's and LQ's heads, and they were presented with a giant check in the amount of one hundred thousand dollars.

She gave LQ a tight squeeze, and then she felt someone's hand on her back. It was Ace.

"As soon as I saw that amazing cake you made, I knew you'd win. Congratulations. You deserve this," he said, pulling her into a gentle hug.

She hugged Ace back, not letting herself savor it the way she'd like to because the cameras were still rolling. "Thanks, Ace. You made me work for it."

Cara and her family came out of the audience to share hugs and kisses with her and LQ. "I knew you could do it! See, the next time I make a prediction, you're going to have to listen to me."

A.J., Cara's husband, kissed her on the cheek. "Now you

can come back home and the kids can have their favorite babysitter back."

At A.J.'s words, Ronnie realized that the fantasy was over. It hadn't been all blue skies and roses, but it had been the best adventure of her life. But now it was over. And that meant it was time to face the realities of her relationship with Ace.

Ronnie handed Cara's baby girl back to her. In a few minutes she and LQ were due for follow-up interviews in the press room. She wanted to touch up her hair and makeup.

As she turned away from her friends, Ronnie was pulled into a hug. "Congratulations, Ronnie."

"Andre. What the—" She pulled away, backing out of his arms.

"I always knew you were a winner. How about dinner to celebrate your big win? On you, of course. You're the one with a hundred thousand dollars," he said, laughing as though he'd just told the funniest joke in the world.

Ronnie scoffed. "You're kidding me, right? You and I aren't friends. Why would I go to dinner with you?"

He leaned in and deepened his voice in the way that used to make her melt. "We *could* be friends again."

Now that tone just made her skin crawl. "No, thanks. Tonight I have my choice of dinner dates, and you're not on the list."

His eyes became cold, and Ronnie braced herself. Finally, she recognized what a cruel person Andre had always been. Whatever he had to stay, she could handle.

"Your choice, huh? I suppose your referring to the Sexy Chef himself. Are you two really a thing? I thought that was just some publicity stunt."

"Whatever we are to each other, it's certainly none of your business."

"Sure, now that you're skinny you can get a guy like that. But you're a chef and you like to eat. Let's be real. You probably won't always be that slim. Where will he be when you gain all the weight back?"

She swallowed hard. "I'm not going to—"

"Maybe you will, maybe you won't. But maybe you should be nicer to me. I'm the only one who wanted you when you were fat."

Feeling her face flash hot with anger, Ronnie opened her mouth, but before she could get any words out, Cara stepped to her side.

"What are you doing here, Andre? Isn't there a rock you should be crawling under?"

Then an arm slid around her waist. It was Ace's. He kissed her on the cheek. And when she turned to look up at him, he kissed her full on the mouth. "Are you ready to go out and celebrate your win? We can do it up big, inviting one and all, or we can make it more of an intimate celebration, courtesy of me, the Sexy Chef," he said with a grin.

Andre rolled his eyes and walked away.

Cara released a big sigh of relief. "Thank God that loser slithered away. I almost died when I saw him over here talking to you. What did he say?"

Ronnie waved him off. "Nothing important. You know Andre, he's full of shitake. Mushrooms, I mean."

"I always hated that guy," Ace said to Ronnie. "Your taste in men has improved a great deal since him."

They all shared a laugh, but inside Ronnie felt a niggling of fear.

She knew that Andre's words had been intended to make her feel insecure. It had been an old tactic he'd relied on in the past to keep her from leaving him. Even though she saw through him now, it didn't keep his words from hurting her.

People who lost a lot of weight often fluctuated or even gained it all back. She couldn't promise that she'd never be fat again. Would Ace still want her if she did gain it all back?

Ace sat in the hotel bar with Marcel and Garett. They'd insisted on buying him a drink, just in case he felt like drowning his sorrows.

"Honestly, guys, I don't feel that badly about the loss. Sure, I would have loved that prize money, but I don't think I stood a chance in the last round. I'm not much of a pastry chef. That area is where Ronnie has always been strong. You saw that cake she made. Mine was okay, but hers was spectacular."

Garett curled his upper lip. "You're just saying that because you *love* her," he said in a mocking tone. "I miss the days when you were a hunter and no one woman was enough for you."

Marcel clapped Ace on the back. "Sorry, buddy, but Ace has finally come over to my side. Team monogamy. One of these days you're going to have to join us."

Garett crossed his arms. "Never. It's not going to happen. All the qualities I need to keep me interested don't exist in one woman. I'm doing them a favor by spreading my love around."

Ace shrugged. "Just make sure whatever you're spreading isn't contagious."

Garett downed the last of his drink and stood up. "All right, you guys don't appreciate me, but I think I see a sexy Parisian girl in the lobby who might."

Marcel stood up next. "Well, brother, we can't win them all. Tomorrow morning Simone and I are getting on a train for Rome, where we're going to gorge ourselves with pasta for three days. See you back in the Big Apple."

They exchanged a handshake and then Ace was alone. Not hearing his name called to win the big check had stung a bit, but he knew just how much that win meant to Ronnie. The look on her face had been worth a hundred thousand dollars.

Maybe now that the competition was finally behind them, they could focus on their relationship. They'd made fantastic memories in Las Vegas, Kauai and now Paris, but he was anxious to see how they would do once they were back home.

They were from two different cities, but Manhattan was only a four-hour drive and a sixty-minute flight from Washington, D.C. That was a workable distance until they could figure out something more permanent.

He didn't want to pressure her right away. Ronnie knew how he felt about her. That was going to have to be enough for him until she grew confident in her own feelings.

Ace headed back to his room, looking forward to calling Ronnie when he got there. He hoped she'd want to stay in tonight. While he loved a good party, after all the stress of the last couple of weeks, a more private party was starting to look good to him.

As he got off the elevator, he saw Ronnie slipping something under his door.

"Hey, Ronnie. What are you doing? Slipping me a love note?" he asked with a smile.

She looked up, startled and somber, and instantly Ace's heart began to sink. Her expression told him that it definitely wasn't a love note.

"Oh! I—I tried to call your room, but you weren't in, so I thought I'd leave a note."

Ace steeled himself. "I'm here now. You can tell me what's on your mind face-to-face."

Chewing her lower lip, she stepped back for him to unlock his door, then followed him inside.

Ace took a seat, realizing he probably wasn't going to like whatever she was planning to say. "Go ahead. What's in the note?"

Ronnie picked it up from the floor. "Do you just want to read it?"

He shook his head. "No, I'm not going to make it easy for you. I want to hear you say the words."

Her brow wrinkled. "What words?"

"That you're dumping me. Right? Isn't that the gist of the note?"

"I'm not *dumping* you," she started, and Ace felt a twinge of hope. "I'm not certain we were ever anything officially anyway."

"Really? It has to be official? How much more official does it get than my telling you that I love you, anyway?"

Ronnie covered her face. "I'm just afraid we're making a big mess of this. The competition is over. We have to go back to our real lives now. I live in D.C. You live in New York. There are so many reasons why we shouldn't drag this out."

"Drag it out? I thought we cared about each other. You already know that I'm in love with you." Watching her face, he saw the skepticism pass over it. "Oh, I see what the problem is. You don't believe that I love you. Listen. I'm thirty-two years old. Don't you think I know my own mind by now?"

"It's not that I don't think you know your own mind. I'm just not sure you want *me*. Sure, I'm thin now. But I wasn't always this way, and I may not always be thin. Will you still love me if I get bigger again?"

"Of course."

She shook her head. "You answered that too quickly. You didn't even take the time to think about it."

"Why do I have to think about it? I love you. It's not a passing fancy. I've known you for years. Do you really think I wasn't attracted to you when you were heavier?"

"No, I don't think you were."

"Ronnie, the last time I saw you before this competition, you were in a relationship. I would have tried to date you, but you were never available. It wasn't your weight that stood in our way."

"Look, thanks for trying to make me feel better, but that's not really what this is about. I've got to stop making the same mistakes over and over."

"You can't possibly be comparing my relationship with you to your relationship with Andre. I know I've always tried to treat you well. Don't you trust me?"

She sighed. "I don't know if I trust *me*. I just can't tell if I've finished all the work I need to do on myself. I'm not sure if I'm ready to be in a relationship. I'm still confusing the wrong things with love."

"So you *do* love me? Ronnie, if you love me, I'm not going to just sit here and let you walk out of my life."

She froze for a second.

"I never said I loved you."

"Are you saying that you don't love me?" Ace asked, watching her carefully.

"Yes, that's what I'm saying."

He should have been hurt, but in that instant, he knew that she was lying. But if she wasn't ready to admit that, then he'd just have to wait. If their love was as real as he felt it was, he knew she'd come back to him.

He'd enter every *Food Fight* that came up to keep her in his life if he had to. But for now, there was nothing more to say. There was only one thing to do. Let her go.

Chapter 20

Ronnie got on the plane to fly home the next day. This time she didn't have time to focus on her fear of flying—she was too entrenched in her own heartache.

Saying good-bye to Ace hurt more than anything she'd ever experienced before. But like the burn of a vigorous workout, Ronnie kept telling herself that the pain was good for her.

Didn't this almost physical pain in her chest where her heart was supposed to be mean that she was growing? In the past, she'd stayed with men in order to avoid this terrible feeling. The fact that she was willing to suffer like this had to mean that she'd finally started doing what was best for her instead of what felt good.

In a few days this pain would fade, she told herself.

In the meantime, she had the glow from a big win to bask in and a huge check burning a hole in her bank account. She could start planning to open another restaurant now. All she had to do was choose a location and a concept.

But as Ronnie returned home and fit herself back into her old routine, she couldn't focus on her dream. It was all she'd wanted when she'd started out in the *All-Star Food Fight,* and now that she'd won the biggest prize of the competition, all she could think about was how lonely she was.

"Come sit down with me for a minute," LQ said, pulling her into a booth before Crave opened for dinner one evening.

Ronnie took in a deep breath. All she could hope was that LQ hadn't found another job. She didn't know what she would do without her.

"What's on your mind?"

"The real question of the day is what's on your mind. You won the *Food Fight,* but you haven't been the same since. We were all prepared to handle you if the fame went to your head, but what do we do now that you've been in a funk for the last week?"

Ronnie gasped. She thought she'd been doing a good job of hiding her feelings. "Has everyone noticed?"

"Of course. It's all anyone talks about when you leave the room. Is it Ace? I thought you were the one who dumped him. Are you having second thoughts?"

She shrugged, trying to make it seem like it wasn't a big deal. "It's natural for it to hurt a bit at first. I'll be fine."

LQ made a face at her. "What are you talking about? You dumped him. Why did you do that if you want to be with him?"

"Because it can't last. We're from different cities. We have different priorities. It just won't work."

"Look, I know I was hard on him at first," LQ said. "But he's kind of proven to be a deeper guy than we all thought. Aren't you supposed to wait for it to *stop* working to decide that it's not going to work?"

"That's been my problem in the past. I wait too long to see that something doesn't have a future. I'm trying to learn from those mistakes."

"You poor mixed-up thing. You've been screwed over so many times you don't know a good man when you find one."

"I know Ace is a good man. But that doesn't mean he's a good man for me. I don't know if I'm really his type. There may come a time, down the road, when he might find me disappointing."

"What on earth are you talking about?"

"Some men love women who are thin. He never showed much interest in me when I was heavy. Who knows what would happen if I gain the weight back one day. I don't plan on it, but it could happen. I don't want that constantly hanging over my head."

"Ronnie, the man told you he's in love with you. Do you honestly think that can be undone by a couple of pounds? Don't you think he's well past that with you?"

"I don't know."

"Can you tell me one thing?"

"What?"

"Do you love him?"

Ronnie swallowed hard. She'd gone out of her way not to say the words out loud. If she said them, she'd have to deal with them.

"I don't know."

"Don't play coy with me, Ronnie. What's the truth?"

Taking a deep breath, she said. "Yes. I love him."

"Then you have to take a chance."

"Why don't you let me fix you up with someone," Garett whispered in Ace's ear as he filled his table with another stack of cookbooks. Ace was at a major Manhattan bookstore chain to sign that day.

"My PDA is full of potential dates for you. All you have to do is tell me what you like. Models, business professionals, a girl-next-door type…just name your poison," his friend continued.

Ace shook his head, then signed his cookbook for an elderly woman who claimed she'd prepared every recipe in his last book. As the woman walked away, Ace craned his neck to glare at Garett.

"I've already told you that I don't want to date anyone in your contact list."

"You don't have to worry. They aren't all women I've dated. Some of them I just got numbers from but never called."

Ace rolled his eyes, then put a big smile on his face for a pair of housewives that were giggling as they approached him. Ace signed their books and joked with them a bit, then turned back to Garett.

"I'm not interested. Let's just leave it at that."

"You've got to get back on the horse. It'll help you forget about Veronica."

Ace rubbed his temples. "I don't want to forget about Ronnie."

"It's over, man. It's time to move on."

"I'm not so convinced about that. But you don't have to concern yourself with my love life one way or the other. Besides, it works better when you stay out of it."

"You say that now, but you're known as the Sexy Chef. That means you have a reputation to live up to."

"You're the only one who thinks so. I don't think my career would suffer at all if I were to get married or have a couple of kids."

Garett pretended that Ace had just stabbed him in the

heart. "Don't do it. It's bad enough that you've been on this monogamy kick lately. Our friendship will die a quick death if you go ahead and get married."

Ace shrugged. "Your day will come. Eventually one of these girls you date is going to get you on the hook. Then there won't be any turning back."

"Stop cursing me. Look how miserable you are. You'd wish that on me?"

"I may be miserable now. But I honestly believe it's temporary. Ronnie just needs a little time to realize that she's ready. I think she's going to come back to me."

Garett paused. "What makes you so sure? What do you know that you're not telling me?"

"That's going to have to remain my secret for now. Maybe when she comes back to me, I'll let you know."

Ronnie was still thinking about LQ's words when she went to the gym the next morning. She'd never been more confused in her life.

Of course she had feelings for Ace. But she'd also had feelings for all the other jerks she'd dated in the past. And staying with them until they ruined her life had been her mistake.

She'd spent so much time distrusting men, it was hard to know when it was the right time to take a chance. Would Ace be like all the rest and break her heart one day?

"You worked out like a madwoman today," Cara said, when they sat down together at the Big Squeeze. "What was motivating all that intense energy?"

Ronnie didn't feel like talking about it so she tepidly said, "My zeal for good health?"

Cara scoffed. "You know I'm not going to let you get away with that. Try again."

Ronnie shrugged.

"It's Ace, isn't it?" her friend asked. "You've been a complete mess ever since you came back from Paris. Maybe you should call him. Talk things out."

"There's nothing to talk about."

"Really? You can talk about why the two of you broke up. Didn't he say or do something to upset you?"

Up until now, Ronnie had been avoiding this topic with Cara. She'd been front and center to all of Ronnie's disastrous relationships in the past. All she'd wanted Cara to see this time was how strong she was being, resisting the urge to go back to a dead-end relationship.

"No, actually he didn't."

Cara's brow furrowed. "Then why did you break up with him? He seemed perfect for you."

Ronnie reared back. "Perfect for me? Weren't you the one warning me off him when I was in Hawaii?"

"That was before we found out what was really going on. You two have always been friends, and now the two of you have fallen in love. Sometimes there's no better way to find your soulmate."

"Now you think he's my soulmate?"

"He could be. Why not?"

"Because there's too much standing between us. There are a lot of obstacles. Maybe we never should have let things leave the neighborhood of friendship in the first place."

"Ronnie, is that how you really feel?"

"The only thing I know is that it wouldn't hurt to be apart from him now if we'd never gotten started in the first place."

"All relationships are a risk. Look, I know better than anyone why you'd be afraid to start over. But just because you've been hurt doesn't mean you can't find true love. Look at A.J. and me. I was so afraid that all men would be like the ones in my life that did me wrong, that I almost ruined things between us. I really made it hard for him. But he was the right guy so he stuck it out. Maybe Ace is the right guy."

Ronnie shook her head. "I'm so confused. I don't know what the right thing to do is. There are a few things that are still bothering me."

"What things?"

"Maybe they're my own baggage or maybe they're real concerns—I don't know how to find out."

"If you care enough about him, you'll go ahead and take the leap."

Ronnie frowned at Cara. "I'm the queen of taking the leap. That's been my problem, remember? I've always given my boyfriends second and third chances to show me that they're the one. That's why I don't know what to do. If I go crawling after Ace, how is that different from all the times when I was a fool for love?"

"The difference is that Ace hasn't broken your heart. You're punishing him for what all the men in your life have done to you in the past. Maybe you're the one breaking his heart."

Ronnie's body went still. Was it possible that she'd broken his heart? He was the one who had told her he loved her, and she had never really said it in return. Was she the villain here?

What if she did try to contact Ace and he didn't want to speak to her? What if she'd hurt him so badly that he'd have nothing to do with her?

For the first time, Ronnie realized that there were more feelings involved in this relationship than just her own. She'd already hurt Ace. She couldn't risk hurting him again when she didn't even know what she really wanted.

Chapter 21

As Ronnie started work the next night, she felt as though she were under a microscope. Was everyone she knew monitoring her moods?

With that in mind, she went out of her way to put on a happy face. But inside she'd never been more confused. Part of her wondered if talking to Ace would help her sort out her feelings. But they weren't going to casually run into each other. They lived four hours apart in separate states. She'd have to make a very deliberate and long trip if she decided she wanted to talk to him again. Talking on the telephone wasn't likely to help her answer any questions for herself.

Dinner service at Crave was going even better than usual, so Ronnie felt good that at least one area of her life was starting to come together. Since the airing of her *Food Fight* win, there had been several write-ups on her restaurant in local papers.

Just as she was in the midst of reverie, her host, Callie, came to the back and whispered to Ronnie. "There's a special diner who's asked to give her compliments to the chef."

Immediately, Ronnie's nerves kicked in. "Special diner? Who is it?"

"Sharon Vincent. She's a writer for *Taste* magazine."

Wiping her hands on her kitchen towel, Ronnie followed Callie into the dining room.

"Ms. Vincent, this is our executive chef and the owner of Crave, Veronica Howard."

Ronnie shook hands with the woman. "Welcome to Crave. I hope you enjoyed your dinner."

Sharon Vincent was a lovely brown-skinned woman with a round face and a slightly plump figure. She was dressed in expensive designer clothes "It's an honor to meet you, Chef Howard. Everything I tried was mouthwatering and delicious, but hands down the best thing I've ever put in my mouth was your chocolate kiss dessert. I wish I didn't live so far away because I'd be back every night for that one."

"Thank you so much. That dessert is our signature dish. I'm so glad you liked it. Where are you from, Ms. Vincent?"

"Please, call me Sharon. I'm from New York City. Any chance you'll be opening a restaurant in the Big Apple?"

Ace flashed in Ronnie's mind. That's where he lived. If she opened a restaurant there, she'd have an excuse to see him all the time. Pushing those crazy thoughts aside, she smiled at Sharon.

"I do plan to open up another restaurant, but I haven't decided on a location yet."

"Oh! I thought for sure you'd come to New York to be close to your boyfriend."

Ronnie blanched. "My boyfriend?"

"Ace Brown, the Sexy Chef. I followed your romance in the tabloids. You'll never find a better guy. I shouldn't have let him get away."

"Get away? Did you date him?"

"You don't have to worry. It's been over for a long time. I'm a married woman now. But, yes, we dated awhile back before he left for his world tour. He left a man who didn't want to settle down and came back looking for a commitment. Of course, I'd moved on by then. But we're still friends. I think you two make a wonderful couple."

Ronnie's mind reeled as she took in Sharon's words. It was highly unlikely that Sharon had put on the extra pounds she carried in the time that she and Ace had been apart. That meant that Ace had dated a woman who was a bit overweight much the same way she had been.

Clearly, Sharon misread Ronnie's stunned expression for jealousy, because the woman was bending over backwards to reassure her. "Seriously, it never would have worked out with Ace and me. The only thing he and I really had in common was a love of food."

"Um, Ace and I aren't together right now."

Sharon's face fell. "That's a shame. I thought I saw a real spark between you when you were on camera together. It didn't work out? Girl, what am I thinking trying to mind your business like this. Don't mind me."

"Actually, we may get back together. I'm hoping we do."

"That's right. Go get your man. You don't want to let that one get away. He's built to last, you know what I mean?"

Ronnie spent some more time speaking with Sharon and walked away from her table that night with more than just the promise of some good publicity for her restaurant. She now had hope for her future with Ace.

She felt like a fool as it dawned on her that she'd almost let her ex-boyfriend ruin her life once again. He'd gotten in her head and found just the right button to push to amplify her insecurities with Ace.

Now she had to find out if there was any chance that he'd still want her. It was possible that she'd already ruined things between them. Or worse yet, maybe he'd already moved on to someone else.

Heading back into the kitchen, Ronnie made a decision. She couldn't afford to waste any more time. Tomorrow was her day off. She had to go see Ace.

Sunday morning Ace had trouble getting out of bed. For the past couple of weeks he'd been putting on a brave face, but today, his false bravado was starting to wear thin.

Maybe he'd been wrong and Ronnie really didn't love him. Perhaps he shouldn't have made it so easy for her to walk away. He'd been able to do it because he'd been so confident that she'd come to her senses. But now he was starting to have doubts.

Dragging himself to the shower, he tried to plan his day. His best friends would be coming over later for dinner, but if he kept feeling the way he did now, he was tempted to cancel. There wasn't anything he liked better than making good food for the people he cared most about. But without Ronnie among those people, he wasn't really in the mood to do it.

Maybe it was time to stop waiting for her to come around and talk to her. Should he call? He wouldn't be able to see her face over the phone. He needed to look in her eyes as well as hear her voice.

Perhaps the best thing to do was jump in the car and just show up on her doorstep. He didn't care if it made him look needy. At this point that's exactly how he was feeling.

He didn't know if he could move on without trying to get through to her one more time.

With a new plan formulating in his brain, adrenaline began to pump through him. Suddenly highly motivated, he started getting dressed. He'd have to cancel his plans with his friends before he left, but at least this way he'd be doing more than sitting home waiting.

Ace had just finished tying his sneaker laces when his doorbell rang. He wasn't expecting anyone, so he looked through the peephole of his door.

Ronnie was standing on the other side, looking decidedly nervous.

He felt as though his knees might give out, and sweat immediately began to bead on his upper lip as his heart rate picked up. Excited, he jerked open the door.

"Ronnie! What are you doing here?"

"Is this a bad time? If it's a bad time I can—"

"What? Come back later? Ronnie, you live four hours away. It's the perfect time. Come in."

She looked amazing, wearing a pair of sexy dark jeans and a turquoise camisole top. Her hair was pretty and framed her face. All Ace wanted to do was pull her into his arms and give her a big kiss.

But he had to hear what she'd come to say first. He believed it was good news. She wouldn't drive four hours to dump him a second time. But she had to say the words.

Ronnie walked into his apartment and took a seat on the sofa. He offered her a drink or a snack, but she was clearly too nervous for any of that.

"I'm sorry to barge in on you like this, but I think I owe you an apology."

He frowned. "For what?"

"I didn't give you a fair chance. I let a lot of things that didn't have anything to do with you, but had everything to do with my own baggage, stand between us. Now I'm just hoping this isn't too little, too late."

"I'm listening," Ace said.

"The first thing I want to tell you is that I *do* love you. I was lying in Paris when I said I didn't."

Ace laughed and Ronnie looked hurt.

"I'm sorry. I'm not laughing at you. I'm laughing because I knew you were lying."

"You knew? Then why didn't you say anything?"

"Because you clearly needed time to work things out for yourself. I was hoping that when you were ready you'd come to me."

"Then I'm not too late? You haven't found somebody else?"

"Somebody else? How could I find somebody else when all I can think about is you? I still love you."

"Then there's hope for us. You want to try to make this work between us?"

"Yes, absolutely."

Ronnie jumped up and threw her arms around Ace's neck. "I'm so glad to hear you say that. I could barely sleep last night wondering if I'd permanently jinxed things with us."

Ace answered by doing the thing he'd wanted to do the second she'd stepped into his apartment. He lowered his mouth to hers, giving her a long, deep kiss.

Suddenly Ronnie pulled her mouth away from his. "Wait a minute."

"What's wrong?" he asked, trying to kiss her again.

"How did you know I was lying in Paris?"

"Remember when you told me you couldn't lie to Cara because you have a tell?"

"Yes?"

"Well, I figured out what that tell is."

Her eyes widened. "What is it?"

"When you try to lie you twist the earring in your left ear."

"Really? Ha! Cara would never tell me what it was."

Ronnie laughed and he laughed along with her.

"So, you were confident that I'd come running back to you, huh?"

"I was at first. But to be honest with you, that confidence was fading fast. In fact, I was just about to get into my car and drive to D.C. to see you. If you'd shown up an hour later, I would have been there and you would have been here."

Ronnie shook her head. "Then I got here just in the nick of time."

Ace pulled her back into his arms.

"I just have one question for you," Ronnie asked, tentatively.

"You can ask me anything," Ace said, concerned.

"What do you think about opening a restaurant together here in New York?"

Ace smiled wide and leaned in to answer her question with a kiss.

* * * * *

Fru·gal·is·ta [froo-*guh*-lee-stuh] *noun*
1. A person who lives within her means and saves money, but still looks good, eats well and lives *fabulously*

THE TRUE STORY OF HOW ONE TENACIOUS YOUNG WOMAN GOT HERSELF OUT OF DEBT WITHOUT GIVING UP HER FABULOUS LIFESTYLE

NATALIE P. MCNEAL

Natalie McNeal opened her credit card statement in January 2008 to find that she was a staggering five figures—nearly $20,000!—in debt. A young, single, professional woman, Natalie loved her lifestyle of regular mani/pedis, daily takeout and nights on the town with the girls, but she knew she had to trim back to make ends meet. The solution came in the form of her *Miami Herald* blog, "The Frugalista Files." Starting in February 2008, Natalie chronicled her journey as she discovered how to maintain her fabulous, single-girl lifestyle while digging herself out of debt and even saving for the future.

THE *Frugalista* FILES

Available wherever books are sold.

HARLEQUIN®

Have you discovered the Westmoreland family?

NEW YORK TIMES AND *USA TODAY*
BESTSELLING AUTHOR

BRENDA JACKSON

Pick up these classic Westmoreland novels...

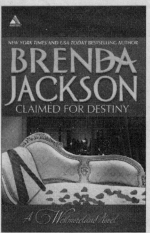

On Sale December 28, 2010

Contains:
Stone Cold Surrender
and **Riding the Storm**

On Sale January 25, 2011

Contains:
Jared's Counterfeit Fiancée
and **The Chase Is On**

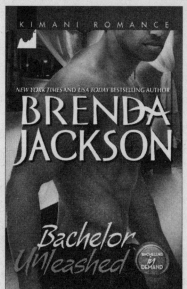

REQUEST YOUR FREE BOOKS!

2 FREE NOVELS
PLUS 2 FREE GIFTS!

KIMANI™ ROMANCE

Love's ultimate destination!

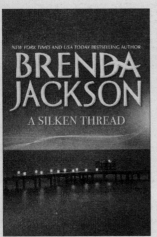